"I'll be glad to see the last of that monstrous emerald."

One of the escorts went through the door first, and Alex saw the man's entire body stiffen.

"Call the police," the guard said as he hurried into the room.

Alex saw Cliff's body lying on the floor at the base of the pedestal. An object he was well familiar with was protruding from a sharp angle out of the guard's chest, a stain of blood slowly spreading on the uniform. The murder weapon was a lighthouse letter opener sent to him by one of his guests.

Buried to the hilt in the man's chest, it looked as if the lighthouse, or at least the image of it, had played a part in another victim's demise.

Reston was standing by, staring at the stone with a grim expression on his face.

Alex patted him on the shoulder. "It wasn't your fault," he said.

"That's not it. Something's wrong."

"What do you mean?" Alex asked.

"This is a fake," Reston said, his voice shaking. "The real emerald is gone."

BOOKED FOR MURDER

Tim Myers

BERKLEY PRIME CRIME, NEW YORK

BOOKED FOR MURDER

A Berkley Prime Crime Book / published by arrangement with the author

PRINTING HISTORY
Berkley Prime Crime mass-market edition / September 2004

Copyright © 2004 by Tim Myers.
Cover design by Jill Boltin.
Cover illustration by Yuan Lee.
Interior text design by Kristin del Rosario.

For information address: The Berkley Publishing Group,
a division of Penguin Group (USA) Inc.,
375 Hudson Street, New York, New York 10014.

Visit our website at www.penguin.com

ISBN: 0-425-19808-1

Berkley Prime Crime Books are published
by The Berkley Publishing Group,
a division of Penguin Group (USA) Inc.,
375 Hudson Street, New York, New York 10014.
The name BERKLEY PRIME CRIME and the BERKLEY PRIME
CRIME design are trademarks belonging to the
Penguin Group (USA) Inc.

PRINTED IN THE UNITED STATES OF AMERICA

10 9 8 7 6 5 4 3 2 1

To Kim, Tom, Natalee, Leslie,
and everyone at Berkley Prime Crime,
For first believing in my lighthouse in the mountains;

To Patty and Emily,
For believing in me;

And most of all
To my readers,
Thanks for visiting the Hatteras West Inn and Lighthouse!

1

"I know I shouldn't admit it, but I'll be glad to see the last of that monstrous emerald," Elise Danton said as she and her employer, Alex Winston, watched the final group of gawkers pass through the lobby of The Hatteras West Inn on their way to see the Carolina Rhapsody Emerald. The spectacular gem was currently being exhibited in one of the guestrooms of the Main Keeper's Quarters, but the show was nearly over.

Alex said, "We were lucky to get it. Reston Shay hasn't had that stone out of his vault in ten years. Look how many folks have come to Hatteras West to see it." Alex owned and operated The Hatteras West Inn, a property nestled in the foothills of the Blue Ridge Mountains sporting a replica of the Hatteras Lighthouse on North Carolina's Outer Banks. The inn's guests stayed in either the Dual or Main Keepers' Quarters; it was a heavy workload for just two people, but somehow they managed well enough. Unfortunately, part of that was due to the inn's constant less-than-stellar occupancy rate.

Elise frowned, her nose crinkling slightly. "These peo-

ple aren't paying guests, Alex. I hate to bring this up, but
that's what we need right now."

He didn't need the reminder; nobody knew the precarious state of their finances better than Alex did. Now that
they had both buildings of the inn up and running at full
capacity, he'd hoped to bring in enough to actually stop
using red ink in his account books, but it hadn't panned out
that way. Emeralds had been found on Winston land by
one of their guests, but the location of the strike had vanished with her when she'd died. The sale of the stones she
had managed to discover had been enough to rebuild the
Dual Keeper's Quarters building after a tragic fire, but
what had once seemed like an abundant source of money
eventually ran out.

"Don't worry. Things have a way of working themselves out," Alex said, wishing he could rely on something
more substantial than hope in comforting Elise. "Let's forget about business for now and enjoy the emerald while we
still can. Reston is picking up the stone in less than an
hour, along with that troop of armed bodyguards escorting
him all over Elkton Falls."

Elise followed Alex as they trailed behind the last of the
crowd to the guestroom where the stone was displayed. It
sat perched atop a glass pedestal resting firmly on an ele-
gant square of lush red carpet directly in the center of the
room. They had moved the furniture out for the occasion,
and the space looked bare without it. In a roped off area the
size of a parking space stood the Carolina Rhapsody, one
of the biggest, deepest green emeralds in the country. As
Alex stared at the glistening stone, he felt the blood surge
in his veins. Alex's great-great-grandfather had been a fa-
mous rockhound in his own right, and the call of the jewel
still ran strong in Alex.

"It is beautiful, isn't it?" Elise said with reverence as
she studied the emerald.

"Breathtaking," Alex agreed. There was a cathedral-like quality to the stone that made him whisper in its presence.

One of the stragglers, a woman from town named Rose Lane who was infamous for her bad temper and curt manner, blocked Alex's view of the stone as she moved close enough to brush against the rope. That brought a big, meaty uniformed security guard with suspicious eyes out of the shadows.

"You'll have to step back, Ma'am," he said in a gruff voice that shattered the hushed tone of the room.

"I just wanted a closer look," Rose said. Her voice bristled with abruptness, daring him to defy her. Rumor had it around Elkton Falls that she'd been too mean to marry, and she'd gotten worse with every birthday.

"Sorry, the roped area is off limits."

She looked as if she wanted to push it, but after studying his bulk and the hard lines of his face, she wisely decided to back off.

Not without a grumble, though. "Why does he display it if he doesn't want folks to get a good look?"

The guard didn't reply, but he also didn't move until Rose was well away from the perimeter. Once she was safely back, the guard returned to the shadows. Reston had been most specific about the display, darkening the room around the emerald and setting up a spotlight that shone down on it like a beam from Heaven. Alex had to admit the affect was worth the man's fussy precision. The Carolina Rhapsody looked absolutely stunning.

As most of the crowd started to leave, Alex approached the guard. "I'll bet you'll be glad when this is over, Cliff." It had taken Alex the entire time of the exhibit to get the man's name, and in all honesty, he still wasn't sure if it was his first name or his last.

In reply, Cliff raised one eyebrow.

Alex filled in, "It can't be easy guarding something worth three million dollars."

The guard said, "It's just another job to me." The man's gaze never stopped as he spoke, going around the perimeter of the room to the windows to the doorway and then back again. From a security point of view, it had to be a challenge keeping track of the many ways to get at the emerald, though Alex knew that the guard's only responsibility was to watch over the stone while it was actually at Hatteras West. Reston Shay's squad picked the emerald up every day precisely at five P.M. and delivered it again the next morning at ten.

"Well, it won't be long now," Alex said as he and Elise left the room.

Someone was waiting for them at the desk of the Main Keeper's Quarters when they walked back into the lobby. Alex suddenly realized he'd forgotten to put up his sign announcing they would be back soon.

"May I help you?" he asked as he took his place behind the registration desk.

The lady in question had brightly dyed red hair pulled back in a ponytail, and wore a floral print dress that matched her flashy running shoes. Over one arm she carried a huge, woven egg basket partially covered with a square of cloth that perfectly matched her dress, and there was the pleasant aroma of baked goods that hovered around her. "I'm Fiona White, and I've got a muffin for you."

"No thanks, I just ate," Alex said, wondering how all the odd birds managed to ultimately wind up at Hatteras West.

Not deterred in the least, Fiona said, "My dear boy, you don't understand. These are free samples to announce my presence in Elkton Falls. I'm opening up my shop in town. I'm the Muffin Lady."

She said the last as if she were announcing the arrival of the Queen.

Elise said from behind him, "We've got a muffin supplier already, but thanks for coming by."

Fiona stood her ground. "You may be under the impression that what you've been serving are muffins, but I've got the real thing." She held back the cloth, and Alex caught a glimpse of the golden brown muffins inside.

As Elise started to say something, Alex added, "What can it hurt? I'll try one."

Fiona smiled brightly as she dove into her basket and pulled out a rich copper muffin the size of a small boy's head. "How about a Pumpkin Delight?" She handed Alex the muffin, then turned to Elise. "And for you, let's see . . . Blueberry Surprise? No, that won't do at all. I try to match the muffin with the person, it's a game I play. I've got it." She reached in and pulled out a yellow muffin with flecks of something inside. "Banana Bonanza sounds like your match."

Elise didn't take the offered muffin, but said instead, "Actually, I wouldn't mind tasting the blueberry."

Fiona laughed with delight. "I knew you'd say that. Here you go. Enjoy."

Fiona watched intently while Alex and Elise tried their muffins. Alex couldn't believe the earthy explosion of pumpkin from the first bite. "What's in this?" he asked as he held the muffin aloft.

"An old family recipe. So may I put you down for a selection of two dozen every morning for your guests?"

Alex was about to agree when Elise said, "We've got a supplier right now who is giving us a very good price on our orders." Truth be told, the muffins Alex got from Buck's Grill were serviceable, but they couldn't approach the ambrosia he held in his hand. He would personally love to have these particular muffins every morning himself for breakfast, but the food at the inn was Elise's area of responsibility, and he was glad to let her have it. He had enough things to keep up with on his own.

Fiona said to Elise, "Why don't you taste your muffin first, then we can discuss terms."

Elise shrugged, pinched off a bit of muffin, then sampled it. If it was anything like the bite Alex had just taken, she would be hard pressed hiding her reaction.

"Perhaps we'll be able to do business," Elise said. "First we need to discuss prices and delivery schedules though."

Alex said, "Why don't you two use my office? I've got some work to do out here anyway." It was no hardship for him to give up his office to them. Alex had been pestered throughout the day by guests treating his private space like some kind of lounge. He'd found Reston Shay there waiting for him that morning, and then not an hour later, after answering a summons from one of the suites, Alex had returned to find Melva Flump tapping her fingernails on his desk, demanding postcard stamps and maps to area attractions.

As Elise and Fiona disappeared inside the office, Alex took another bite of the pumpkin muffin. It was just as good as the first had been. He saw Elise's blueberry muffin sitting on the registration desk and decided to sneak a bite to see if it matched his own.

It turned out that Elise had missed her calling; she should have been an actress. The blueberry was very nearly better than the pumpkin.

He trusted Elise to make the best deal for them, but even if she decided Fiona was too expensive for the inn, Alex knew he wouldn't be able to resist buying one now and then for himself.

Twenty minutes later, with the Muffin Lady long gone and the final work for the day completed, Alex found Elise taking inventory in their supply room.

"Busy?" Alex asked as he watched her go through the checklist on her sheet.

"Give me one second," she replied as she continued with her work. Alex smiled in admiration. Elise's inventory system was part of their increased efficiency at Hatteras West since she had come onto the scene. Alex shuddered slightly as he remembered life before her arrival. Elise's predecessor—her cousin Marisa—a born crier if ever there was one, had nearly driven him crazy with her constant tears. With Elise on the scene, his world had settled into a blissful routine of competence. However, his heart had been thrown into turmoil since then, too. They had tried a disastrous date the month before, a debacle that still stung. There was still something between them, there was no doubt about that, but finding their way to what it might be was more perilous than he'd expected. Dancing the fine line between love and friendship was proving to be difficult. Someday, someday soon, he was going to ask her out again, and this time he planned to be better prepared for it than he had been before.

At last she finished her list. "Okay, what can I do for you?"

Alex said, "I wanted to see if you were interested in one last look at the Carolina Rhapsody before Reston gets here."

"You never get tired of staring at it, do you? I suppose it wouldn't hurt to get one more look." As she spoke, there was a loud clamor out front, and Alex realized they'd waited too long.

Reston was in the lobby, along with his entourage.

The dapper fellow said, "There you are. We're getting ready to move the stone for the final time. Want one more peek before we do?"

"That would be great."

Reston offered Elise his arm, and she smiled slightly as she took it. It was obvious the older man still considered himself a temptation. As Alex followed behind them, he heard Reston say to Elise, "If you'd like, you may hold the emerald for a moment."

"Thanks, but I'd be too afraid I'd drop it."

"Nonsense," Reston said, "If something should happen, which I'm sure it won't, the emerald is fully insured. I insist."

Elise nodded. "I'd love to, if you're sure."

"Absolutely," Reston said as they neared the room.

One of his escorts went through the door first, and Alex saw the man's entire body stiffen.

"What's wrong?" Alex asked as he tried to see around the bulky form.

"Call the police," the guard said as he hurried into the room.

Alex held off obeying the order. After all, he couldn't bring Sheriff Armstrong up to speed if he didn't know what had happened himself.

Reston looked ashen as stumbled into the room, Elise's arm released and forgotten. Alex saw Cliff's body lying on the floor at the base of the pedestal. An object he was well familiar with was protruding from a sharp angle out of the guard's chest, a stain of blood slowly spreading on the uniform. The murder weapon was a lighthouse letter opener sent to him by one of his guests.

Buried to the hilt in the man's chest, it looked as if the lighthouse, or at least the image of it, had played a part in another victim's demise.

"The emerald is still there," Alex heard one of the guards say as his partner checked for a pulse.

The man kneeling beside Cliff shook his head after finding none. "He's dead."

Alex decided it was time to make that call to the police. He found Sheriff Armstrong in his office, and quickly secured the man's assurances that he'd soon be out there along with Doc Drake and Irene Wilkins, Elkton Falls's beautician/crime scene specialist. Alex hung up and returned to the room where the emerald was being displayed.

As Alex walked in, he heard Reston saying, "This is all

my fault. I never should have taken the Carolina Rhapsody out of the vault. It's cursed."

One of the guards said, "Cliff knew the risks of the job. I'm disappointed in him, though," he added as he looked down on the body.

"Why is that?" Alex couldn't help himself from asking.

"The blade went into his chest. He let his guard down with the wrong person. It was obviously someone he knew."

Alex agreed with the logic of it. "Are you an off-duty cop or something? You don't look familiar."

The big man shrugged. "My name's Skip Foreman. I was a deputy sheriff in Mecklenburg County before I retired up here for the peace and quiet."

The other guard said, "Skip, come take a look at this."

"Excuse me," the big man said as he joined his partner.

Reston was standing by, staring at the stone with a grim expression on his face.

Alex patted him on the shoulder. "It wasn't your fault," he said.

"That's not it. Something's wrong."

"What do you mean?" Alex asked.

Instead of answering, Reston stepped over the rope and plucked the stone off its pedestal. Reston examined the gem a moment, then said, "Somebody stole the Carolina Rhapsody."

"It's right there in your hand," Alex said.

"This is a fake," Reston said, his voice shaking. "The real emerald is gone."

2

That got Skip's attention. "Hang on a second, Mr. Shay."

Skip pulled a plastic baggie out of his pocket and said, "Slide it in here."

"Why bother? I'm telling you, it's a fake," Reston said.

Skip said patiently, "If that's true, that glossy surface is perfect for fingerprints."

Reston did as he was told, and Skip secured the possible forgery in his pocket.

"Now what do we do?" Reston asked as Sheriff Armstrong rushed in. The man had been on a diet for the last three weeks, grumbling at the world but determined to fit back into his old uniform before the next election.

The sheriff asked, "What have we got here?"

Skip identified himself, and Alex saw Armstrong grimace. The sheriff said, "You're not looking for a job are you? We've already got a sheriff in Canawba County."

Skip shook his head. "I just took this job as a favor for a friend. I'm retired, sheriff, and I don't have the slightest desire to get back into law enforcement."

Armstrong looked relieved by the admission. "Naturally, I'd be glad to have your input on this case."

As the two men conferred, Alex noticed that Elise had left the room. He was torn between hanging around to see what he could find out and going in search of his maid to offer his comfort.

Elise won, with barely a flickering glance back at the body.

Alex found her sorting sheets in the laundry room. "Sorry you had to see that," he said as he took a sheet and started folding it himself.

"I am too, but death is a part of an innkeeper's life," she said. "It's the sad, honest truth that people die just about everywhere."

Alex thought about it a moment, then said, "Maybe you were right, though. I should have turned Reston down when he asked to display the emerald here."

"Nonsense," Elise said. "That man's death had nothing to do with Hatteras West."

"I wish I could believe that. Did you happen to see the murder weapon?"

Elise paled slightly. "It was the letter opener Rosemary sent you."

"I just hope she never finds out what happened to it," Alex said, remembering the sweet and lovely young lady who came to Hatteras West every year to get away from her normally glamorous world of high fashion in New York City.

Alex and Elise finished their folding and emerged into the lobby in time to hear Doc Drake tell the sheriff, "There's nothing I can do here. I'll fill out the death certificate this afternoon, but it's pretty cut and dried. I need to get back to the office or Madge is going to roast me. I left her with a waiting room full of patients."

The sheriff nodded and Drake took his leave.

Elise touched Alex's arm and said, "I have some things

to do over in Dual," referring to the second of two buildings that made up the inn. The Dual Keeper's Quarters had recently been opened to the public again, and they'd found it had become necessary to split many of the tasks they used to share.

Alex said, "I'll find you after this is all cleared up."

After she was gone, Alex took a chance and asked Armstrong, "Sheriff, what's going on?"

Armstrong said, "Shay keeps claiming the stone's a fake, but it looked real enough to me. I put in a call to Hiddenite for Jasper Hanks. I figure he can tell me whether it's the real thing or not."

"Do you know anything more about Cliff?" Alex asked.

"I didn't realize you knew the man," the sheriff said.

"He's been at the inn all week. We had a chance to chat every now and then." That was at least partially true, though Alex had been the only one doing the talking during their conversations.

Armstrong nodded. "All I can say for sure at this point is that the letter opener probably killed him."

Irene Wilkins, the beautician/criminologist, approached with a shiny bag in her hand. Irene was becoming one of the leading county criminologists in their part of North Carolina. She'd become so popular with the other forensic experts around the state that she was being called away to work on cases farther and farther from Elkton Falls. Her police duties were taking so much of her time that Irene had actually been talking about taking on a partner in her beauty shop.

Armstrong said, "What have you got there?"

"I found this in the guard's pocket." She held it up to the light, and Alex saw a small, tarnished yellow rock.

"What's that supposed to be?" Armstrong asked.

"Unless I miss my guess, it's a raw gold nugget," Irene said.

"Gold? The closest anybody's ever found gold to Elkton Falls is near Charlotte at the Reid Gold Mine, and that's at least an hour and a half away." He turned to Alex and asked, "What was it doing on the floor in there?"

"I don't have a clue," Alex said. "I've never seen raw gold before in my life."

Armstrong asked, "Any chance that's fool's gold, Irene?"

"No way, Ducky. Once you've seen the real stuff, iron pyrite will never fool you."

Alex said, "You sound like you know what you're talking about."

Irene admitted, "I've been known to pan for gold a time or two myself. It's a hobby that gets me outdoors, and besides, sometimes you find something worth the cost of your trip. I've panned in Georgia and here in North Carolina, too. Probably taken half a pound out of the water in my day."

Armstrong said, "We'll get Jasper to look at it, too."

"Ducky, are you saying I don't know gold when I see it?" There was an edge in Irene's voice that challenged him to defy her.

"No, Ma'am," he backpedaled. "I'm just saying, for the record and all, I need something in writing from an expert. You say it's gold, so gold it is."

"Get your written report then," Irene said. "I've done all I can in here, and I'm sure Alex would like us to hurry things along."

"I'd appreciate it, but don't rush on my account," Alex said.

She grinned at him. "I never do, you know me better than that, Alex."

Irene disappeared back into the room with the body to collect her equipment while the sheriff went off to find the EMS folks. Alex tagged along with Armstrong, and as soon as the techs were given the green light, they went in to collect the body. Alex knew that their service had a business arrangement with Elkton Falls to transport dead bodies when the occasion arose, charging a flat flee for each trip to the hospital morgue.

Standing on the porch as the crew loaded the body into the back of the ambulance, Alex noticed a figure walking up the drive toward them, and he and the sheriff watched intently as the man approached. It was Patrick Thornton, another guest at the inn, and Alex wondered how in the world he was going to explain what had happened without running the man off. As he got closer, Alex could see that Thornton was dressed as usual in heavy work boots, a thick canvas pair of pants, sturdy shirt, and worn leather hat. There was a stained and battered backpack hanging from the man's shoulders, and a notebook tucked under one arm. In the other hand he held a scarred walking-stick that nearly reached his chin. He had a rugged, worn look about him, as if he'd spent the vast majority of his life out in the sun and under the stars.

"Afternoon," Thornton said. "Something going on here I should know about?" he added as he gestured to the ambulance.

"There was an accident," Alex said as the sheriff nodded his greeting as well. It wasn't quite a lie, but Armstrong wouldn't let it stand. "More like a murder, Alex."

"That's too bad; the world's a hard place sometimes." The outdoorsman offered his hand to the sheriff and said, "I'm Patrick Thornton."

"Armstrong," he replied curtly as he offered his hand.

Thornton turned to Alex and said, "Has that check arrived?"

"Not yet," Alex said.

"Blast it all, they should have fired that infernal secretary a month ago. She fouled me up in Lenoir last week, I don't know why I thought this week would be any different."

Alex said reluctantly, "If it's not in today's mail, I'm

going to have to start charging your room to your credit card." He'd agreed to settle for an imprint of the man's card upon check-in, but it had been two days and there was still no sign of the promised check to cover his week's room rate.

"I understand completely. Now if you two will excuse me, I need to drop this pack off in my room."

After Thornton was gone, Alex explained to Armstrong, "He's with the Geologic Survey Foundation, whatever that is. They're checking map coordinates for the Department of the Interior. His secretary was supposed to make reservations for him before he got here, but I never heard from her."

"Sounds like your tax dollars at work, doesn't it?" Armstrong said.

The surveyor was in his room less than ten minutes before he came out again. Alex and Armstrong were still on the porch, discussing the day's events.

Thornton asked, "Can you call a taxi for me, Alex? I need to see this mayor of yours to make sure my permissions came through."

"Our taxi service is kind of sporadic," Alex admitted. "All we can do is call Rebecca and see if she's free."

Irene came out and joined them, her kit in her hand. "Let's go, Ducky."

Armstrong hitched up his trousers. "Well Alex, I guess we're finished here. You can have the room now."

"Thanks, Sheriff. Do you happen to be heading back into town?"

"Sure thing, I've got to drop Irene off at the beauty parlor."

Alex said, "If you don't mind, my guest could use a ride."

"I don't want to put you out," Thornton said.

"Don't mind a bit. I'm heading to Town Hall myself

anyway after I drop Irene. Can't promise to get you back out here when you're done, though."

"It's really not necessary," Thornton said.

"Come on, you can keep me and Irene company. We ran out of things to say to each other a long time ago."

Irene said, "Just because I've heard all of your stories doesn't mean I've told you all of mine."

"I'll give you a dollar for every one you haven't blabbed to me a hundred times before," Armstrong said.

"Get out your checkbook, Ducky, I'm eating dinner at Monet's Garden tonight, on you."

Before they could go, Alex asked, "Have you eaten there yet?"

Irene said, "They just opened up last week, Alex. I heard Irma Bean had a fit during their grand opening, but if you ask me, it's about time she had more competition than Buck's Grill. I've heard this Monet fellow is really nice."

Armstrong huffed, "I've heard he kisses all the women's hands, if you can believe that. A little too rooty-tooty for Elkton Falls, if you ask me."

"I don't remember anyone asking you anything, Ducky," Irene said.

As the three of them walked to the cruiser, Armstrong and Irene traded barbs while Patrick Thornton trailed along behind them like a lost puppy. Alex realized that he might not have done his guest any favors by snagging him a ride with the sheriff. Sitting in the backseat while those two sparred might have been more trouble than hooking up with Elkton Falls's on-again off-again taxi service.

It would certainly have been a quieter ride, even with Rebecca Gray rambling on as she wheeled her truck toward town.

Alex went back to the guest room that had been serving as a display area to get things back in order. It would take an hour or two of work to make the room fit to rent again, though there wasn't a pressing need for the space. The inn was operating just a little better than half-full. Still, if things should take a drastic turn for the better and more rooms were suddenly needed, he wanted to be sure he was ready.

Alex was surprised to find Reston Shay still in the room, standing alone in the shadows and staring at the empty pedestal. Sheriff Armstrong had taken the gemstone, fake or otherwise, from Skip and had promised to return it to Reston when the investigation was complete.

Alex coughed, then said, "I'm sorry to bother you. Just let me know when you're finished in here."

Reston looked up at him, and from the glaze in the man's eyes, it was obvious he was lost in his own thoughts. "Alex," he said as he recovered, "I still can't believe it happened."

"I know. You can't blame yourself."

"For the theft? Why on earth should I do that? I took every precaution for the Carolina Rhapsody's safety, surely you can see that."

Alex said softly, "I'm talking about the guard's murder."

Reston stared at him a second more, then nodded. "True, that's the real tragedy here, isn't it? The emerald never was alive, was it, not that different from any other rock in the ground." Reston raked both hands through his hair, then locked his fingers behind his neck. "Some folks say that stone is cursed. Up until now, I never believed them."

"Why should it be cursed?" Alex asked. He'd been around rockhounds all his life and he'd never heard anyone say one word about the Carolina Rhapsody.

"It's been hushed up, but the Rhapsody has claimed a victim or two before today. Tristan Glenn was the first owner, and the first to die from it. He was holding the stone in the palm of his hand when he died, did you know that?"

"He had a heart attack," Alex said. "It had nothing to do with the stone."

"Perhaps," Reston said, "but how do you explain his wife? Three months after she inherited the stone, she took her own life."

"I don't know anything about her," Alex admitted, "but couldn't it be she missed her husband, or maybe she had other problems? An object can't be cursed, Reston."

The older man sighed, then said, "If it is, the stone is someone else's worry now. I was getting ready to sell it, did you know that?"

Alex was taken aback by the news. "I didn't have a clue."

"That curse has been in the back of my mind since I bought it. Truth be told, I was eager to get rid of it. Fifteen years was long enough for me to own it."

"Is that why you never displayed it?" Alex asked.

"Are you asking me if I was nervous that something like this might happen? I just never figured it would harm anyone but me." Reston stood, looked at the stand for another few seconds, then added, "I suppose one way of getting rid of it is as good as the next. Either way, it's not my worry any more."

He hesitated at the stain on the floor where Cliff had been slain, then gingerly stepped over it and paused at the door.

The sooner the room was cleaned and brought back into circulation, the better Alex would feel.

He didn't believe in ghosts, despite what others had said about The Hatteras West Inn, but he also didn't want any reminders around that tragedy had visited the place again.

"I'd like to get started on the room, if it's okay with you."

"Sorry, but I can't let you touch a thing, Alex. My insurance man is on his way." Reston glanced at his watch. "In fact, he's late. I can't wait around here all afternoon.

When he gets here, show him anything he wants to see. If he wants me, he can track me down himself."

"I'll be glad to help any way I can. Do I have your blessing to straighten things up after he's finished?"

"Knock yourself out," Reston said, and then left.

Ten minutes later, Alex was at the front desk going over the reservations for the following week when a thin man with enormous glasses came into the inn. Alex always knew when his guests were coming, and though some walk-ins made it out to the isolated inn, most folks reserved their rooms in advance.

"May I help you?"

"Are you the proprietor?" the man asked.

"I am. I'm Alex Winston."

The man ignored Alex's outstretched hand and put a business card in it instead. "Parker Worth Moore" was inscribed on it in raised letters. "I'm with RPS. We underwrote the insurance for the Carolina Rhapsody. Could you show me the room please?"

Alex led him down the hall and used his passkey to unlock the door. "We had the emerald on top of the pedestal," he said.

The man frowned at him. "If you'll excuse me, I'll be ready to interview you later."

Alex took the dismissal and backed out of the room. Twenty minutes later, the insurance man returned to the lobby. He barely asked Alex three questions before he left. What an odd little man, Alex thought. Before Moore could leave, Alex asked, "Is it okay if I clean up the room now?"

"My investigation of the scene is concluded, but I may have more questions for you and your staff later."

"Fine," Alex said. After the man left, he decided to dive into the cleaning and make things right again as soon as he could. Maybe with the pedestal removed and the furniture back in the room, he'd be able to put the ugly murder and theft out of his mind. Hatteras West deserved better.

3

Alex was cleaning the floor, scrubbing the last of the bloodstains from the wood when he spotted something against the baseboard. They had all missed it in their previous searches of the room, including Irene, but that was easy to understand. The small, flat square of gray metal was the size and thickness of a dime; it blended in with a floor grate that was almost the exact same color, nearly disappearing.

Alex picked the metal up, held it in his hands and studied it. There were crisscrossing lines etched in its surface, embedded in lightning-strike patterns. The edges were polished smooth. It was the oddest thing Alex had ever seen. Putting it in his shirt pocket, he promised himself that he would show it to Armstrong when he came back out to the inn. Most likely it belonged to one of their guests long before the guard was killed, but Alex would show it to the sheriff just in case.

Elise found him scrubbing the floor a few minutes later. "Let me do that, Alex."

He studied the faded spot, gave it one last swipe, then

said, "That's as good as it's going to get. Do you have some free time? I'd really like to get this room in shape."

"That's why I'm here. With all the furniture crammed into number 4, we're losing two rooms."

"Let's do it then."

As they carried the bed-frame back to its rightful place, Elise said, "Alex, there's something I've been meaning to talk to you about."

"Go ahead. I'm a captive audience right now," he said, pinned against the wall by the metal frame.

"We've discussed this before, but I really think it's time we changed the way we name our rooms," Elise said. "I know your grandfather and father set things up this way, but that doesn't mean it's the only method available, or even the best one."

"Elise, if we renumber the rooms, I'll never be able to find anything. What's wrong with the order they're in now, anyway?"

"It's not the order, Alex. I think we should do away with numbers altogether."

Alex raised one eyebrow. "How are we going to keep track of our guests without room numbers?"

"I think we should come up with names for each of the rooms. It's more personal that way."

Alex said, "So you think staying in 'Bob' is better than number 7?"

She frowned slightly, then said, "Alex Winston, are you making fun of me?"

"Maybe a little," he admitted hastily.

"Alex, you know perfectly well that I don't want to call a room 'Bob.' But how about the Jasmine Suite? We could have a Carolina Room, a Foothills Retreat, a Keeper's Rest, the possibilities are endless."

"I like those names better than 'Bob,' I'll grant you that, but I'm still not sure we need to make a change."

"Alex, I don't want to keep harping on this, but we need

guests, and if we can make the place feel more charming in our brochures, we might have a better chance keeping things afloat."

Alex stared out the window at the lighthouse, collecting his thoughts before he trusted himself to speak. "I guess a lighthouse in the mountains isn't enough of a pull any more, is it?"

She moved beside him, put her hand on his shoulder and said softly, "Alex, trust me, they'll fall in love with the lighthouse, but we have to get them here first. If you're against renaming the rooms, I won't push you about it."

He thought about it for another full minute, then said, "Why not? Let's do it."

Elise nodded, "That's great." She paused, then added, "I don't know how we can keep from having an Emerald Room even with what just happened, but it should probably be in the other building."

"I don't want anything at Hatteras West to remind me about what happened today."

Elise said, "We can talk about it later. Does the sheriff have a clue about what happened?"

"If Armstrong does, he's not telling me. Reston's positive the stone's a fake, and I'm not one to doubt him when it comes to his own emerald. He thinks it's cursed, you know."

"That doesn't surprise me. You know the stories about the Hope Diamond, don't you?"

"Now don't you start," Alex said. "One believer around here is more than enough for me."

"I didn't say I believed it," Elise said, and Alex felt relief until she added, "But I didn't say I didn't, either. Well, I'd better get back to cleaning my rooms."

As Alex put the last of the furniture back in place, he moved the rug that had been there before and covered the ghost of a stain still on the floor. The pedestal was outside in the hallway, along with the remnant of carpet it had sat on. Reston had brought both pieces with him, and Alex realized he'd have to go into town to return the man's property, since it was doubtful Reston Shay would ever step foot in Hatteras West again.

But Reston was still at the inn, sitting on the front porch of the Main Keeper's Quarters in one of the rocking chairs, staring up at the lighthouse.

"I thought you'd already gone," Alex said as he put the base and the carpet down beside the rocker.

Reston shrugged. "If you want to know the honest truth, I don't feel much like being alone right now."

Alex said, "I can certainly understand that."

Reston took a deep breath, then said, "Alex, do you have a spare room out here? I might just stay on a while. I find myself with a real need for company."

"We've got room for you," Alex admitted. "Not that I'm not glad to have you, but are you sure it won't be too painful for you, staying here where the emerald was stolen?"

"On the contrary, I believe I'll be able to deal with the loss better if I'm right here. I know it might sound morbid, but is there any way I can stay in the room where it was taken? Don't ask me why, but I'd feel better being there. Besides, my insurance man will probably be out again later, and it's not fair to keep you from income I know you need."

As they walked back inside, Alex said, "Don't worry about me. The room is yours for as long as you want it."

Elise was checking the reservation book out front as they came in. "Mr. Shay," she said, "I'm so sorry about your loss."

"Thank you, my dear."

She stood there in slience, uncertain about what to do until Alex said, "Reston is going to be staying with us for a while. He's requested the same room."

Elise bit back her surprise, but Alex could see it flash

across her face. "Of course," she said as she led them back to the room.

"I'll have my people bring a few things out later," Reston said. "For now, I think I'd like to be alone for awhile."

Alex and Elise went back down the hall after he closed the door, holding their conversation until they were sure he could no longer hear them.

Elise said, "He wants to stay in that room? Tonight?"

Alex said, "I know, I don't get it either. But hey, he's paying for the privilege. I wasn't about to tell him he couldn't stay there."

"You did the right thing, but I still don't get it," Elise said.

As they neared the desk, Alex asked her, "So, will we be having fresh muffins in the morning?"

"They always are, aren't they?" she replied.

"Come on, you know what I'm talking about."

Elise smiled gently. "I've agreed to try the Muffin Lady's offerings for one week, strictly on a trial basis. After that, we'll see."

Alex said, "As long as I get a pumpkin one every morning, I'll be happy."

Elise laughed. "Don't worry, that was one of my first conditions."

Alex smiled softly at her. "Outstanding." He took a deep breath, then said, "Speaking of food, have you heard about the new restaurant in town?"

"Monet's Garden? Everybody's buzzing about it, especially Irma Bean. She's afraid it's going to put her out of business."

"Nonsense," Alex said. "Folks are ready for a change of pace, but they'll come back to her, you mark my words. Anyway, I was wondering if you might like to try Monet's with me tomorrow night?"

Elise's brow crinkled. "Are you asking me out on another date, Alex? Wasn't the last one disastrous enough for you?"

"Come on, we said we'd try again. We don't even have to call it a date if you don't want to. Just two people going out to dinner, enjoying each other's company."

Elise thought about it a moment, then said, "I don't care what we call it. It sounds like fun."

Alex grinned at her and said, "It's a date, then." Before she could reply, he said, "Kidding. I'm just kidding."

She said seriously, "Maybe a date is exactly what I'd like to call it." Elise started to walk off, turned and added, "Now you'll have to decide if I'm kidding or not. See you later."

He was still trying to figure it out when the newly wed Pendletons walked into the inn. From the look of the storm clouds on Mor and Emma's faces, all had not been blissful during their time away.

"She wants to keep Sturbridge, if you can believe that," Mor said, scowling at his bride. "After all the trouble that creep caused while he was alive, he's still meddling in my life beyond the grave."

Emma said, "Oh, pooh. Mor Pendleton, I've been Emma Sturbridge for so long I don't know if I'd ever manage as Emma Pendleton."

"And why not?" the big man rumbled. "Pendleton is a fine name."

Evidently their argument had been going on since the two had said their vows. They'd extended their honeymoon an extra two weeks after hearing that Toby Sturbridge's killer had been caught, and Alex had missed them in their absence.

Elise came in, hugging Emma and Mor at the same time. "Welcome back, you two. How was the cruise?"

Emma said, "It was delightful. Three weeks at sea does a body good."

"Me, I'm glad to be back home," Mor said. "Les is going crazy trying to do everything by himself. He's been threatening to change the name of the place to 'Just Les, No Mor No More.' "

"How clever of him," Emma said.

"Woman, you're just trying to get my goat, and I'm not going to give you the satisfaction. Okay, you had to say hello to Alex and Elise. Now can we go back to my apartment and unpack?"

"Your apartment?" Emma asked. "I naturally just assumed we'd be taking up residence in my cottage when we returned."

"That place is all sharp angles, I'll kill myself there. What's wrong with my apartment?" he asked.

"Nothing, if you like neighbors surrounding you from all sides. Now my cottage has all the room you could need. Don't worry, you'll get used to living there in no time."

Alex said, "You could always stay here until you decide where you're going to live. We'd love to have you."

"Sounds good to me," Mor said, then a second later Emma added, "It's sweet of you to offer, dear friends, but we'll work this out. Mor, are you coming?"

"If you could tell me where we're going, it might help," he said, winking at Alex out of Emma's line of sight.

"It's a surprise," Emma said.

"I don't like the sound of that," Mor added as the door shut behind them.

Alex looked at Elise, and both of them started laughing at the same time. Alex said, "I don't envy them the decisions they're going to have to make."

Elise said, "Don't kid yourself, they're going to enjoy every minute of it. We should take them with us to Monet's Garden, kind of a welcome back gesture."

"A double-date," Alex pretended to consider it, fighting to hide his smile. "I don't know about that. I kind of hoped to have you to myself."

"Oh, Alex, you're hopeless."

"I do my best," he said as she headed back toward her room.

Armstrong called later that night just as Alex was heading off to bed.

"I didn't wake you up, did I?" the sheriff asked.

"I'm just getting around to closing the inn for the night. What's going on?"

"I thought you'd like to know what's been happening, seeing how it all took place out there at your inn," the sheriff said. "Jasper Hanks just left my office. Remember, I told you he's my gemstone guy from Hiddenite."

"What did he have to say?"

"Turns out the emerald really is a fake. It's nothing but pretty glass. When you match it to a picture of the Carolina Rhapsody, they don't look all that much alike, not up close, so just about anybody could have had it made. The gold's real, though. Still can't figure out how it ended up in Cliff's pocket."

Alex said, "So where does that leave things?" He had to catch himself from saying, "where does that leave us." That would bring Armstrong's truculent side out and would most likely cut off Alex's supply of information.

The sheriff said, "I need to start digging around in the usual places. Reston Shay's got to be a suspect, since it was his stone stolen, but I can't rule out the folks in Cliff's life either. I know the stone is most likely the main reason he was murdered, but somebody might have just considered it a bonus. I doubt it, but it's a possibility I've got to follow up on."

Alex asked, "Do you think the murderer planned this for awhile, or was it spur of the moment?"

Armstrong was silent for a few seconds, then said, "To be honest with you, I think it was a little bit of both."

"I don't follow," Alex said.

"Think about it. The murder weapon was right there at the inn, so it's not like that was planned out in advance or anything. On the other hand, we've got to consider the fake. It looked enough like the Carolina Rhapsody to fool most folks unless you got up close to it, so there had to be some planning involved. I can't imagine somebody just walking around with that thing in their pocket. When's the last time you saw the real thing? Or could you tell?"

"From a distance? No, but as close as I was to it, when Elise and I saw the emerald this afternoon it looked like the real thing to me. That was around three, I guess."

"So between three and five P.M., somebody snuck in, killed Cliff, and stole the emerald. Any suspicious folks hanging around the inn over the last few days?"

"Nobody comes to mind."

"Did anybody check in or out today?"

"Slick and Nancy Hickman checked out early this morning before all this happened. They had to head back to West Virginia. Oh, I almost forgot. There was also a woman who came by. She called herself the Muffin Lady. She was here sometime around four, I guess. "

Armstrong laughed. "Yeah, I know all about her. She was handing out muffins in town yesterday, and causing a whale of a traffic jam at Five Corners. Sometimes I wonder what Elkton Falls is coming to, what with this new restaurant opening up and the muffin woman showing up, too."

"Hey, I guess some folks call it progress," Alex said as he stifled a yawn.

Armstrong caught it and said, "Well, I'll let you go. I just thought you'd like to know what was going on. Alex, you keep your nose out of this and I'll touch base with you every now and then. But if you start snooping . . ." He let the phrase hang in the air.

"No problem," Alex said. "I've got enough to do running this inn."

"Then we understand each other. Good night, then."

"Good night," Alex said as he hung up the telephone. He hadn't been entirely honest with the sheriff. Alex wasn't about to let it go completely, though he didn't plan to do any active digging. He still had a vested interest in the murder and theft; after all, they had both happened on Winston property. In a very real way, that made it his business.

Too late, Alex remembered the odd metal token he'd found in the room where the murder had taken place. He thought about calling Armstrong back, but then decided to wait till later. Most likely it wasn't a clue at all, probably just a discarded piece from someone's travel game.

He'd have to talk to Reston the next day about the Carolina Rhapsody, and try to find out who might have been behind the theft. It was a puzzle that would most likely lead to discovering the killer.

4

The next morning, Alex stared at the amazing glut of muffins on the continental breakfast bar they put out for their guests and asked, "Elise, did you forget to cancel the muffins from Buck's this week while we're trying the new ones?"

It was easy to tell the Muffin Lady's products from Buck's; they were twice the size of their standard fare, towering over Sally Anne's offerings like bullies on the beach.

Elise said, "I talked to Sally Anne last night, but she brought more this morning on her own. She said she wasn't giving up that easily."

"I'd better call her and make sure everything's okay between us," Alex said, reaching for the telephone. Doing business in a small town was very much like working with family. He saw Buck and Sally Anne at their diner at least three times a week, and if this new Muffin Lady drove a wedge between them, no matter how good her baked treats were, it wasn't worth losing two of his good friends.

Just as he'd dreaded, Buck answered the phone at the

diner with a grumble. The man was an ex-boxer, and while he and Alex had always gotten along, that was one side of Buck that Alex made a point to avoid.

"Buck, it's Alex."

There was silence on the other end of the line, and Alex held his breath waiting for Buck's pronouncement.

The big man said, "Listen, we need to talk."

"Okay, I'm willing to do just that," Alex said. He took a deep breath, stalling for time to come up with some way to deal with the situation.

It was a good thing he had. Buck continued, "Sally Anne told me she pushed more stuff on you this morning, and I explained to her that wasn't how we did business. It won't happen again."

"Listen, this isn't personal. You know how I feel about you two."

Buck said, "Alex, you run a business, just like I do. Do you think I get mad at everybody who doesn't eat at the grill?"

"Is there anybody in town who doesn't?" Alex asked.

Buck laughed, producing a gentle thunder. "Don't kid yourself, there are plenty of folks who don't come in here at all. So let me ask you this right out in the open. Are you ditching us, or are you just shopping around for another supplier? We'll still see you for lunch, won't we?"

"I'll be by there soon," Alex said. "This whole muffin business hasn't been decided, Buck. We're just testing the waters."

"Whatever you do is fine with me." There was another pause, and Alex could almost hear the frown in the big man's voice as he added, "Sally Anne's new at this end of the business. The deliveries to the inn are her baby. You might have some trouble with her. It wouldn't hurt to talk to her."

"I'll come by this afternoon," Alex promised as he hung up the phone.

Elise had followed Alex's half of the conversation. "Well? What did he say?"

"Buck understands, but Sally Anne's a little upset about the situation."

Elise said, "Alex, I didn't mean to cause trouble between you'all. Buck's muffins are fine."

He shook his head as he grabbed a pumpkin muffin from the basket. "We're not going to run this inn afraid of every step we take, Elise."

Reston Shay came into the lobby and was the first in line for breakfast.

"Did you sleep well?" Alex asked him, honestly curious about the man's stay in a room that had so recently hosted a murder.

"Like a kid," Reston said. "I try not to let the world intrude on my rest, no matter what happens."

"Do you think there's a chance you'll ever get the Carolina Rhapsody back?" Elise asked.

"It's probably on its way out of the country by now," Reston said. "Some fool collector is probably going to buy the thing knowing it's hot and hide it, I just know it."

Reston grabbed a muffin, one of the bigger ones, along with a cup of coffee. "I need to make some calls right after breakfast. I told the sheriff last night, so I don't suppose I'm jumping the gun sharing it with you. I'm putting up a reward for the return of the emerald, for what good it will do, and another one that leads to the arrest of the murderer. Cliff might have let his guard down, but he was still killed while he was working for me, and I take care of my own people."

"That's good of you," Alex said.

After Reston disappeared back into his room, Elise asked, "Do you really think the emerald's out of the country?"

"I wish I knew. Reston's probably right, though. It

makes a lot more sense for some collector to buy it and keep its possession a secret."

"What good is it to own something if you can never show it to anyone else?" Elise asked.

"I understand that adds to the thrill of it all for some folks," Alex admitted.

"Well it sounds strange to me. If there is a curse on the emerald, I hope it turns around and bites the new owner, hard."

Tracy Shook, the newly elected mayor of Elkton Falls, walked into the inn with a scowl on her face.

Alex said, "A frown this early in the morning? Don't tell me the mantle of being mayor is already weighing you down."

"There are more headaches than I bargained for, that's for sure. Is Reston Shay staying out here with you?"

Alex nodded. "We just saw him. What's up?"

"I'm not thrilled about these rewards he's publicizing all over town. It's liable to shake a lot of nuts from the trees."

"News travels fast," Alex said. "We just found out ourselves."

"Reston told Armstrong, and Armstrong told me. The kudzu vine didn't have far to travel this time."

After Tracy headed off to Reston Shay's room, Elise asked, "Are you still interested in trying that new restaurant tonight?"

"Sounds good to me. I feel kind of sneaky though, going there behind Irma's back."

Elise said, "She's got to expect that at first. After all, she's been the mainstay in town for a long time."

Alex nodded. "Okay. Are you still determined to invite Emma and Mor along?"

"Come on, Alex, it will be fun."

He shrugged. "Hey, if it's the only way I'm going to get you out on the town, I'll take it."

She laughed gently. "I'll invite Emma and Mor first, then I'll make the reservations."

"Then I can have another muffin," he said as he reached for a cranberry one.

"Shouldn't you save those for our guests?"

"I suppose so. You're no fun at all." He looked longingly at the muffin again, then said, "Well, if I can't eat anything else, I might as well get to work."

"You poor thing," Elise said.

"That's what I keep telling you."

With the opening of both buildings of the inn, Alex and Elise had taken to splitting their lunch hours so someone would be available for their guests. He missed the odd meals they'd shared together before, but with the added rooms came a renewed set of responsibilities. He let her eat first, putting off the trip into town and his dreaded meeting with Sally Anne.

Finally, after Elise had been back over half an hour, Alex drove into town to see if he could smooth some feathers.

Buck's was fairly deserted by the time Alex walked in. He'd hoped to blend in with the crowd, but it looked like he'd be facing the duo alone in the spotlight.

Buck was at the counter reading the paper, and Sally Anne was nowhere in sight. "Where's your daughter?"

"She had a dentist appointment." He grinned as he added, "I was worried about handling the crowd myself with her gone, but I'm managing."

Alex asked, "Is the new place hurting business?"

Buck frowned. "They're not taking much of my trade away. Irma's the one I'm worried about. She's taking all this pretty hard. I keep telling her folks will come back, but she's not so sure. Have you eaten at the new place yet?"

"No," Alex admitted, reluctant to confess that he had reservations for that night.

"Well don't feel bad about it when you do. Just try to go to Irma's pretty soon, okay? She could use the company."

"Is it as bad as that?" Alex asked.

Buck stood and folded the paper. "Probably not, but she's feeling that way. You want the usual?"

"Sounds good. I'll just sit here at the bar with you." As he took a stool, Alex added, "Are you sure we're okay about this whole muffin thing?"

Buck said, "Alex, business is one thing, friendship is another." The big man put a meaty paw on Alex's shoulder. "You and I are fine."

Alex nodded and picked up the discarded paper as Buck disappeared to make his club sandwich. As he leafed through the *Charlotte Observer*, a familiar face caught his gaze in the obituaries. It was for Cliff, and as he read the guard's requiem, Alex was surprised to find that the man's parents had possessed an odd sense of humor; either that, or an incredible lack of imagination. The guard's legal name was Clifton Clifford Cliff. Alex searched the obit for any reference to the jewel theft, but it just mentioned he'd died suddenly.

In the end, that about summed it up.

Sally Anne came in as Alex was halfway through with his sandwich. "Good afternoon," she said primly as she put on her apron.

"Hey there," Alex replied, trying to keep his tone light. "Everything check out okay with that smile?"

"It was just a cleaning," she said as she busied herself wiping down the counter. Alex had been about to get himself a refill for his empty tea glass and wondered what he should do now. There was something about the sweet tea at Buck's that made it the best in town, even including the fancy blends their resident tea expert Evans Graile brewed. Buck had conveniently disappeared in back, so he wasn't going to be any help smoothing things over.

Alex tapped his glass once on the counter, but Sally
Anne chose to ignore it.

This was getting ridiculous. If a few muffins meant the
end of a friendship, he was ready to cancel the whole thing
and go back to business as usual.

Alex had a sudden thought. "Sally Anne, I know you're
upset about the new arrangement, but I've got an idea.
How about if we make it a fair test. You bring half your
normal order this week and we'll put the muffins side by
side. Whoever moves the most muffins wins. Is that okay
with you?"

Sally Anne nodded, then added with a slight smile,
"That's all I ask, a fighting chance." She grabbed a pitcher
of tea and filled Alex's glass without further provocation.
"Thanks, Alex."

"Thank you. And Sally Anne, remember, you're not
going to get rid of me that easily. I'd starve if I didn't have
you guys."

She smiled brightly. "I told Dad you weren't mad at us,
but he wouldn't listen to me."

Alex looked up to see Buck eavesdropping from behind
his order window. The big man offered him a broad wink
before he ducked back into the kitchen. It felt good to
dodge another crisis, at least for the moment.

Since Alex was in town, he decided to stop by Shantara Robinson's General Store to pick up more soap. It was
remarkable how quickly his guests went through his supplies.

"Hey there, stranger, I was beginning to think you forgot your way to my store," Shantara said with a smile.

"Things have been kind of crazy lately." Alex collected
enough soap to last him till his next bulk order came in,
then he noticed a new display in front by the cash register.
It appeared the Muffin Lady was cutting a wide swath
through town.

"She's got you hooked, too?" Alex asked.

"I'm trying them out. Anything to help the bottom line," Shantara said.

"Having any luck so far?"

"Are you kidding? I had a couple from Atlanta come through yesterday and buy me out. They're really good."

Alex nodded. "She's bringing them out to the inn, too. I wonder what brought her to Elkton Falls."

"I never asked. Why?"

"Well, of all the places she could have started her business, I'm just surprised she came here."

Shantara said, "Maybe she likes lighthouses in the mountains."

"You never know."

As Shantara recorded Alex's purchase in her book, she asked, "So, when are you and Elise going out again?" The two of them had been friends since kindergarten, and Shantara freely meddled in Alex's life. He had to admit, he took the same liberties with hers.

He tried to hide his smile as he said nonchalantly, "As a matter of fact, we've got a date tonight."

Shantara whooped with delight, causing a few of her customers to turn and stare at them. If she noticed it, she didn't comment. "So you're taking another step up to the plate. Good for you."

"Don't get your hopes up. It's kind of a celebration for Mor and Emma's return."

"Hey, don't kid yourself. It's still a date."

"You never give up, do you?"

Shantara smiled. "Now what fun would that be?"

"So how's your love life lately?" Alex asked as he took the offered bag of soap.

"Slow, my friend, very slow. I don't mind though, it gives me a chance to catch up around the store."

"Hey, maybe I could fix you up with someone. You could join us tonight and we can make it a party."

She shook her head. "I think you've got enough to worry about without meddling in my life." Shantara paused, then said, "Sorry to hear about what happened out at the inn yesterday. Any leads?"

"I'm staying out of it," Alex said firmly.

Shantara cocked one eyebrow. "And I'm running for prom queen."

"You've got my vote," Alex said as he headed out the store.

"Bye, Alex, and good luck."

"Right back at you," he said as he walked out the door.

Shantara knew him too well to believe Alex was going to stay out of the murder investigation entirely. But what could he do? He hadn't seen anything suspicious around the inn the day before, and there didn't appear to be a single clue. Maybe if the sheriff turned up anything, it might give Alex something to go by, but for the moment, there was nothing for him to investigate. Alex glanced at his watch and saw that the afternoon was quickly passing him by. He had work to do back at the inn before his dinner with Elise and their friends that night.

Maybe, just maybe, it would be the start of something new between them.

5

"Wow, it's hard to believe this place is in Elkton Falls," Emma said as the four of them walked into Monet's Garden. Alex had to admit it was quite stunning, especially when he recalled the dark service bays of the garage before it had been converted into a restaurant. Mr. Monet had created nothing short of a miracle, transforming the space into a light, airy restaurant with hanging plants and wall murals that reminded Alex of Claude Monet himself. In the background, Alex heard a fountain trickling as orchestral music played softly along with it. The place was full of diners, and Alex recognized most of the folks from town. Sandra Beckett, his one-time girlfriend and longtime attorney, was eating dinner in one corner with an older woman who appeared to be a law client, and Alex nodded to her. Sandra smiled brightly back and waved, something Elise didn't miss. "Why don't you go say hello?" she asked gently.

Alex said, "No thanks." He looked around the restaurant for the maître d', but no one was in sight. "I wonder what's holding up our table? Maybe we should just seat ourselves. I'm sure it would be okay."

Mor slapped him on the shoulder. "Smooth, Alex, smooth. That was one of the nicest segues I've ever seen."

"Oh, quit picking on him," Emma said. "Can't you two boys behave yourselves for one evening?"

Mor asked, "Why should we start now? Elise, in case this clod hasn't told you yet, you look dazzling tonight." Alex had to admit it was true. She wore a simple black dress that fell just above the knees, one that accentuated her gentle curves, and she'd done something with her hair, most of it twisted into an exotic braid coiled on top of her head. Her brown eyes shimmered in the light of the restaurant, and it was obvious she was enjoying the opportunity to dress up. It was in stark contrast to the blue jeans she usually wore. Alex sometimes forgot just how stunning Elise could be after seeing her around the inn waxing floors in faded denims and old work shirts. Alex, on the other hand, always felt out of place whenever he wore the one suit he owned. He was born to dress casually, and he felt lucky he'd found a way of life that allowed him to do just that.

Elise smiled softly. "Thanks. I still can't get over your tans. You two must have stayed out in the sun the entire time."

Mor said, "Are you kidding me? Emma wouldn't let me sit down for three minutes at a time before she marched me off to some ruins or open market, and I've got the blisters on my feet to prove it. It was like taking a honeymoon with a drill sergeant."

"You had a good time, admit it," Emma said.

He grabbed her for a quick but intense hug, then said, "Of course I did. By the way, you look pretty smashing yourself tonight."

Alex said, "How about me? I cleaned up pretty good too, don't you think?"

Mor raised one eyebrow. "If you're waiting for a compliment from me, my friend, I wouldn't hold my breath."

Elise flicked a microscopic piece of lint from Alex's lapel and said, "Don't listen to him. I think you look rather handsome."

"Me too. I mean you. You look great," he said, the words tumbling out in a rush.

Mor started to comment, but a quick dig in the ribs from Emma and he bit it back. Elise laughed softly and put a hand on his arm. "Thank you, kind sir." She looked around the restaurant and said, "This really is a treat."

A distinguished-looking slim, older gentleman in a tailored charcoal gray suit returned to the front and selected four menus before approaching them. He had a thick black mustache, though his head was clean-shaven. To Alex, his tanned pate gleamed as if it had been buffed with car wax.

"Welcome to Monet's Garden," he said with a flourish, bowing gently as he greeted them. "Is this your first visit with us?"

Emma said, "Absolutely. We've heard wonderful things about you. About the restaurant, I mean."

He took her hand in his and his lips came within an inch of kissing it. Alex couldn't believe it, but Emma started to blush. She stammered out, "We couldn't wait to try the cuisine here. We've all heard rave reviews."

"It is kind of you to say so. I am the humble owner."

"It's nice to meet you, Mr. Monet," Mor said, shifting between his bride and the restaurateur. He shoved a meaty hand into the host's and said, "I'm Mor Pendleton. Her new husband," he added briefly.

Monet took his hand and shook it, ignoring the jibe, then turned to Alex and said, "And the other happy couple?"

Alex stammered, "We're not a couple. I mean, we're not married. But we're together. For tonight, anyway."

Elise shook her head gently, then said, "I'm Elise Danton, this is Alex Winston. He owns The Hatteras West Inn."

Monet applauded, much to Alex's surprise. "I've heard about your little lighthouse. I must visit it soon."

"It's a full-scale twin made by the same crew used on the Outer Banks for the original," Elise said tersely before Alex could get the words out.

"But of course it is," Monet said. "And now, your table."

He led them to a spot directly beside the fountain, showing them to one of the few tables open. "I trust this will be satisfactory."

Mor mumbled something, but only Alex was standing close enough to hear it. "If you've got raincoats it will be fine."

Alex couldn't believe it, but his best friend was jealous. He wondered if Emma had caught it, but she was probably too busy watching the owner as he walked away to greet another couple.

"He's marvelous, isn't he?" Emma said.

"Certainly different from the norm around here," Elise said.

"How can you not be captivated by the essence of the place?" Emma asked her.

"I want to sample the food before I make any judgments," Elise said. The lighthouse remark had stung her as much as it had Alex. Little lighthouse, indeed.

Mor slapped the table. "I'm with you. He puts on a good show, but the food's the thing."

Emma shook her head slightly, but didn't say anything. A wise decision, Alex thought, considering the storm clouds brewing over Mor's brow.

Elise opened her menu, then said, "Let's see, what looks good."

Alex studied the right side of the menu and was startled by the steep prices. He didn't have to wonder how Monet could afford the fancy décor any more. Buying two meals would cover most of the plants on display and no doubt part of the fountain as well! Alex ordered the least expensive steak on the menu and promised himself he'd cut back on his personal salary at the inn, though he didn't have a clue how he could further trim the meager pay he allowed himself every month.

When it came time to order, Elise chose a modest selection of salmon, while Emma and Mor made more extravagant choices. The repair business had to be bringing in more than the inn, that was certain.

Mor looked nearly apologetic after they'd placed their orders, then explained, "We had a little left over from our honeymoon budget."

Even Emma said, "At this rate, we won't have it for long."

Elise said softly, "Can a place this pricey survive in Elkton Falls? Unless the food is wondrous, I don't think Irma's got anything to worry about."

There was some kind of ruckus going on in the kitchen, filling the air with arguments and accusations. When Monet emerged, his calm and cool exterior was gone, replaced by a blanching of his deep tan. Alex could swear the man's mustache even seemed to curl down at the edges.

It seemed to take forever for their order to arrive. Mor said, "Anything going on new with the Carolina Rhapsody theft or the guard's murder?"

Emma said, "Mor Pendleton, we agreed not to discuss that over dinner."

Mor said, "You agreed, I don't remember having much say about it. Besides, if you see any food, I'll shut right up, and that's a promise."

Alex said, "Reston's claim that the emerald was fake was backed up by an expert from Hiddenite. The sheriff is still trying to figure out how Cliff let somebody get him from the front. He wasn't exactly the most trusting soul I ever met."

"No doubt it was someone he knew," Mor said.

"That's what everybody's been saying, but who could it have been?"

Elise said, "I think it's good you're leaving it up to the sheriff this time."

Alex said, "Hey, I never ask to pry into these things."

He was spared the need to comment on the disbelieving expressions on his companions' faces as the waitress finally brought their food.

She said, "I'm so sorry," as she slid their plates in front of them. Alex's steak was burned to a crisp, accompanied by a sculpture of cold mashed potatoes and the sorriest looking vegetable medley he'd ever seen in his life. He wasn't sure what cut of meat the steak had started off as originally, but it was entirely unrecognizable now. As he tried to chew a bite, he felt his jaw grow numb from the effort.

He whispered to Elise, "How's your fish?"

"Overcooked and overseasoned," she said simply. Elise herself was a wonderful cook, and she acted as if the food was an insult. She'd taken one small bite, then pushed her plate away.

Emma and Mor's choices weren't much better, and the four suffered through the meal trying to make their conversation more appetizing than the food before them. More folks than the foursome were unhappy about their meals, though most of the other diners were just as busy pretending it wasn't dreadful.

Monet came around after the check arrived, a worried look on his face. "Dear people, how was your meal?"

Alex was trying to find something good to say when Mor said, "It was barely edible."

Emma dug him in the ribs, but Mor protested, "Hey, he asked."

"Dear lady, your husband speaks the truth. My chef quit abruptly this evening, and I'm afraid his replacement is woefully inadequate. Please, accept my apologies." He took their check and shredded it in front of them, then slid a card across the table to Mor. "This entitles you to a meal for the four of you at another time, with my compliments. I've been in touch with my employment agency in Charlotte, and they assure me I will have a top chef here by tomorrow night."

Emma said, "Don't worry, everyone will give you another chance."

The owner walked away, a beaten man. Alex said to the others, "I'll meet you all outside."

As the rest of his party left, he approached Monet. "Listen, don't let this get you discouraged. Things happen when you work with the public; believe me, I know."

Monet said, "I swear to you, this venture has seemed jinxed from the very start. I should never have come to Elkton Falls."

"Just think what you would have missed," Alex said, trying to lighten the man's burden. "Mor or Les's repair shop is worth the trip alone, and we won't even mention my lighthouse. You really should come out as soon as you get the chance. I'll give you a guided tour myself."

Monet managed a slight smile. "How do you Southerners manage to deal with adversity with such elegance?"

"Who knows, maybe it's because we've had a lot of practice. Don't give up," Alex said as he gestured around the restaurant. "This is all worth fighting for."

Monet grabbed Alex's hand and pumped it hard. "Thank you for taking the time to speak to me. At least I feel I have one friend in Elkton Falls now."

"Give us a chance, we'll all grow on you sooner or later."

Alex caught up with the rest of his group outside of the restaurant, standing in the emptying parking lot waiting for him. Before Mor could ask him about the delay, Alex said, "Anybody want to go to Irma's? I'm still hungry."

Elise said, "I don't have the nerve to go over there after we deserted her tonight."

Emma said, "Thanks anyway, but we need to get home."

Alex asked, "And where exactly is that, these days?"

"We're staying at the cottage," Emma said.

"For now," Mor added abruptly. "It's just temporary until we can work something out." Alex nodded, and Mor protested, "Hey, we had to have someplace to stay, didn't we?"

"Sure thing," Alex said as their friends walked away toward the cottage.

After they were gone, Elise said, "I wonder if he knows they'll never leave now."

"I've got a feeling he does," Alex said. "So what do you say, should we brave Mama Ravolini's despite everything?"

Elise shook her head. "We've left our guests alone too long as it is. Tell you what, why don't we swing by the grocery store and pick up a couple of steaks? You can grill them out back while I throw a salad together. It's got to be better than what we had in there."

"That sounds great to me," Alex said.

Shopping with Elise was lots of fun, and they added a half gallon of chocolate fudge swirl ice cream to their basket for dessert.

Things were quiet enough back at the inn for them to have a nice little dinner outside on a picnic table near the back of the Dual Keeper's Quarters; the nights were beginning to turn chilly again. As they watched the stars after their meal, Elise shivered slightly in the breeze.

"Are you cold?" Alex asked.

"No, I'm fine," she said.

Alex slipped off his jacket anyway and draped it over her shoulders.

"Now you'll get cold," she protested.

"Are you kidding? I love this temperature."

She pulled the lapels of his jacket together and said, "It's a shame about the restaurant."

Alex nodded. "I don't know how he'll make it, even after he gets a decent chef in there. I'm not afraid to admit it; those prices were too rich for my blood."

Elise said, "And most of the rest of Elkton Falls most likely. He could be counting on the tourist trade."

Alex laughed. "If that was his plan, he should have talked to me first. I'm still waiting for tourists to find our inn."

"That's why we need those new brochures telling everyone about the new room names."

Alex laughed. "I give up. We can rename them in the morning."

Elise said, "Why wait till then? It's a perfect night for a fire. Let's go."

They moved inside and Elise returned Alex's jacket. Instead of putting it back on, he said, "I've had about all of this tie I can take. I'm changing back into jeans."

Elise laughed. "As much as I enjoyed tonight, I'm ready to get back to normal myself."

They met again five minutes later in front of the fireplace. Alex lit the tinder when he'd arrived in the lobby a minute before her and was rewarded with the crackling as the flames caught. Elise had added a blue patterned sweater to her jeans, and her fancy hairdo was gone, replaced with the ponytail he preferred. Alex felt his heart skip yet again at the sight of her. There had to be something he could do to get closer to her, but he didn't know what it could be for the life of him.

Elise grabbed a pad from the Scrabble table and said, "Okay, let's come up with some names."

It was more like a party game than a job, and after an hour of laughter and fun, they'd come up with a list of more names than they needed.

Alex said, "Now we just need to get someone to make the signs for us."

Elise said, "I've already got that covered. Amy Lang's going to do them for us."

"Out of steel?" Alex asked. Amy was Elkton Falls's resident sculptress, and her tastes normally ran to huge outdoor epic works instead of delicate indoor signs.

"No, she's going to paint them on wood blanks she made. She's got quite a fine hand at script."

Alex had seen some of the prices on her sculptures. "How much is all this going to cost us?"

Elise smiled. "We're bartering. She's getting three rooms at the inn during one of our dead weekends. It's a bargain."

Alex thought about all the work that would be involved with the swap, but he did want the signs to look professional. "It sounds like you've got it covered then, so let's go ahead."

Elise leaned over and kissed his cheek, adding a quick hug before she broke away.

Alex said, "Not that I'm complaining, but what was that all about?"

"For trusting me to help run this inn, for taking me out tonight, for everything."

Alex said, "You're most welcome."

He was about to lean forward to offer his own thanks in the form of another kiss when Reston Shay breathlessly broke in on them, looking for all the world like someone who had just seen his own ghost.

6

"Reston, what's wrong?" Alex asked.

"I thought I . . . no, it had to be my imagination," he stammered out.

"What did you see?" Elise asked gently.

"Someone was outside my window just now. But it couldn't have been him. No, I must have been dreaming."

Alex asked, "Who did you see?"

"Cliff." Reston expelled the name of the dead guard as he slumped down onto one of the chairs near the fireplace.

"Let's move you into another room," Elise said. "It can't be healthy for you to stay there."

"Do you think I'm crazy?" Reston snapped. "It was just a dream; it had to be."

Alex said, "We've got plenty of rooms available right now. Tell you what, why don't we put you in the other building?"

Reston stood on shaky legs as he said, "It was a mistake telling you about what I saw, or more likely what I thought I saw. I'm fine now. It just seemed so real."

"All the more reason to move," Elise said.

"I'm staying right where I am," Reston said, then walked with firm resolution back to his room.

"Alex, he shouldn't be staying there, tonight of all nights," Elise said.

"What can I do? I can't very well make him change rooms. He's obviously determined to stay there."

Elise shook her head. "I don't understand why."

"Reston Shay is eccentric, at least that's what everyone says because of his money; otherwise they'd just call him crazy. He's been known to do some of the oddest things over the years."

"Like what?" Elise asked.

"Let's see, there was the time he stood out in front of the bank downtown and handed out ten-dollar-bills to whoever wanted them. I heard he went through three grand before Armstrong made him stop."

"How could the sheriff make him stop giving his money away, no matter how crazy it looked?"

Alex smiled. "It was, according to our fair sheriff, an unlawful assembly without a permit. From the reports I heard, there were a thousand people waiting around impatiently when the sheriff broke it up."

"Why would he give his money away like that?" Elise asked.

"Reston said he was tired of paying the government all he had to in taxes, so he might as well spread it around a little on his own. I almost forgot. On his sixtieth birthday, he hired the Naked Chicken Dancers to entertain at his party. Reston threw it for himself at the park for all of Elkton Falls. I don't know if you've heard of this group, but they dress up in costumes of plucked chickens and cartwheel around, dancing to their own odd music, all the while squawking their heads off."

"I suppose the sheriff broke that one up, too."

Alex laughed. "He couldn't. City Hall had issued the permit for one public birthday party plus entertainment, so there wasn't a thing in the world he could do about it. I think Reston just sees the world from a different angle than the rest of us."

"But none of that explains him staying in that room. It's downright creepy."

Alex said, "I couldn't agree more. Tell you what, first thing tomorrow I'll see if I can get him to switch. Now where were we?" Alex asked as he moved closer to her.

Elise yawned, then said, "I was just off to bed. Thanks for tonight, Alex. I'll say this, it's never dull when you're around."

Alex had been hoping for at least a good-night kiss, but he took solace in the fact that this date hadn't ended in complete and utter disaster like their last one had. Maybe there was hope things would improve, if he just kept trying. One thing was certain; Alex wasn't about to give up on Elise.

The next morning, Alex was sampling a cranberry muffin from the Muffin Lady when Elise joined him.

She said, "Sorry I'm late. I didn't mean to sleep in."

"You're entitled to, every now and then," Alex said.

Elise surveyed the continental breakfast bar and said, "How's the muffin race going?"

"Sally Anne's not going to like it, but there's no doubt we've got a new supplier. Patrick Thornton took two, with my permission, so he wouldn't have to stop for lunch. They're a meal in themselves, aren't they?"

"I was a little worried about their size, but our guests seem to like them. Where is our surveyor off to today?"

"He told me he'd be sticking close to the inn. He says there are some spots on Bear Rocks he needs to check out, and more in the orchards between here and Amy's." Though Alex's property was separated from the sculptor's by an orchard of trees one of Alex's ancestors had planted, she was still his closest neighbor at Hatteras West, at least as the crow flew. It took longer to drive there than it did to walk, given that he had to go over three sides of a square to get to her by road.

"Have you seen Reston this morning?" Elise asked. "I wonder if the poor man got any sleep at all last night."

"You can call Reston Shay a great many things, but poor shouldn't be on the list."

Elise lowered her voice. "How did he acquire his money, do you know?"

"All of Elkton Falls does. His family bought my family's land four generations ago in Hiddenite and mined it until there was nothing left."

"Oh, Alex, I didn't know. I'm sorry."

"Nothing to be sorry about. If my great-grandfather hadn't made that first strike, then sold his land and traveled to the Outer Banks, he never would have met my great-grandmother and I wouldn't be here. Neither would the lighthouse, for that matter." Alex had told Elise early upon her arrival how the lighthouse had ended up in the foothills of the Blue Ridge Mountains, a monument to his ancestor's love and devotion for his wife. It was the ultimate of grand acts, one Alex was proud to be heir to.

She said, "You've got a point there. I think I'll check on him anyway, just in case."

Alex said, "I'd let him sleep in, if I were you. Don't worry, Elise, I'm sure he's fine."

She bit her lower lip as she looked down the hallway toward Reston's room, but Alex was glad that she gave up the idea of waking the man. There was enough to cope with at Hatteras West without worrying about a cranky Reston Shay.

Alex was halfway through with his rooms when Elise popped in. He asked, "Hey, what's up?"

"Would you like a hand with your workload?" she asked.

"I must be slowing down. I knew you were quick, but that's got to be some kind of record."

Elise snagged a dusting rag from Alex's cart and said, "You have twice as many occupied rooms as I do, and some of mine aren't even up yet. Reston Shay doesn't answer my knock," she added pointedly.

"With the night he had, he'll probably sleep in until noon."

Together, they tackled the room he'd been working on, knocking it out in record time. Alex loved working alongside Elise. The two of them had an almost psychic connection, splitting tasks without conferring, and working with mechanical precision.

"So let's talk about it," Elise said as they moved to another room.

"What, our big date?" Alex asked with a grin. "I knew it, you can't wait to go out with me again, can you?"

"The Winston charm notwithstanding, I was talking about the murder and the theft."

Alex pretended to sigh. "And here I thought this was going to be about me."

"Oh be serious," she said as she flipped a towel at him.

"Okay, I guess I could give it a try, but I'm not making any promises." His good mood was definitely showing.

"Suspects, Alex," Elise said as she started on the bathroom. It was a game they'd played often enough in the past, discussing the possibilities of the crimes that came their way.

He thought about it, then said, "Well, I'd say we have to start off with anyone desperate enough to kill for money. That stone was a rarity."

Elise shook her head. "That's what doesn't make sense. Why steal something you can't sell? I imagine the Carolina Rhapsody is recognizable to anyone in the trade."

"With collectors, you never know what might drive them. I don't have a single suspect to name based on avarice," Alex admitted. Did he really want to play this game with Elise, when what he wanted was to pursue a personal relationship with her? "We're just going to have to leave this one up to the sheriff."

"I don't believe you actually feel that way for one second."

Alex realized she wasn't going to let go. After working side by side with her, he knew Elise's stubborn streak was wider than his own.

He said, "Okay, here goes. I think Reston's got to be on our list."

"You're kidding," Elise said. "Why would he steal his own emerald?"

"If he took it himself, he gets the insurance and still gets to keep the gemstone."

Elise said, "But why kill Cliff? He could have staged a robbery easily enough without killing someone."

Alex nodded. "You've got a point. Okay, who else do we have? It could be one of the other guards, say Skip for instance."

"An ex-cop killing a security guard? I don't see it."

"We just have his word that he's an ex-cop," Alex said. He thought a bit more, then said, "Okay, if you don't like him for it, how about Fiona White?"

Elise stopped working and stared at him. "Now you're accusing the Muffin Lady of homicide? On what grounds?"

"She was here around the time of the murder," Alex said.

"So was our surveyor, Patrick Thornton. You might as well accuse Rose Lane while you're at it; she was here, too."

Alex said, "Hey, wait a minute. I think you might have something there."

"Now you're saying that Rose might have killed Cliff? Come on."

Alex said, "She's connected with Reston in some way,

I can feel it in my gut. I'll have to ask Hannah Parsons about it."

"The bookstore owner in town? Why would Hannah know?"

"She's been around Elkton Falls forever, and she never forgets anything. I bet you she could tell you who she sold nearly every single book to since she's been open for business."

"Okay, I'll take your word for it. Is there anybody else you want to add to your list?"

Alex thought about it a few seconds, then said, "No, that just about covers it so far."

"I should hope so."

Alex shrugged. "That's why I think it's impossible to do anything until we have more information. There's just not enough to go by yet."

Elise ran the vacuum, then asked, "What do you make of the gold Irene found in Cliff's pocket? It's not exactly a normal token folks carry around with them."

Alex said, "I admit it; I'm stumped by that. Now if it had been some kind of gemstone, too, I might have wondered if it had something to do with the emeralds buried on my land, but the closest gold around here is nearly two hours away."

"You mean the closest that we know of," Elise said. "You didn't think there were any precious gems around here before, either. Could there be gold on your land as well?"

"If there is, nobody I've ever talked to has found any, and I certainly never heard my folks mention it. I'll talk to Emma and see what she thinks." One of Emma Sturbridge's jobs was acting as Alex's resident gemhunter. Though they suspected there was a vein of emeralds somewhere on Winston land, its location had remained a secret, despite Emma's best efforts. During the hard times since the discovery, Alex had toyed with the idea of shutting down the inn and searching for the gemstone vein in earnest, but the voice of reason always pulled him back. After all, finding a fortune in gems had done nothing to enhance his great grandfather's life, and Alex didn't doubt for one second the discovery could cause more problems than he was willing to cope with. He knew the gemhunter in Hiddenite who discovered the Carolina Queen had been forced to hire armed guards to stand watch over the site around the clock. The last thing Alex wanted to do was to live in an armed camp, because he was staying put at Hatteras West, no matter what. The tower meant too much to him, was too great a presence in his life, for him to ever leave it. He glanced out the window and looked up at the beacon; steadfast and loyal, ever present. The lighthouse could use a fresh coat of paint, but other than that, The Hatteras West Lighthouse was in as good a shape as the day it was completed. While the lighthouse on the coast had suffered through riser and handrail problems because of heavy foot traffic, his own had been inspected and given a glowing seal of approval by the same structural engineers who had worked on the coast. The team had booked the inn for a week while they studied his lighthouse, with the single condition that they not make a single modification to his tower. The crew had been like kids swarming over the structure, delighted to find it in such pristine condition. Alex guessed that having a limited number of visitors had saved his stairs, though it nearly broke his pocketbook.

Elise came up by his side, and said softly, "Hey, remember me?"

"Sorry, I was just thinking about the lighthouse."

She nodded. "I've got an idea. Why don't we take a picnic lunch up there today? The view should be spectacular."

"That sounds great to me," Alex said.

Elise said, "Now about that nugget. We don't know about Rose Lane or the gold in Cliff's pocket. Is there anything else we're leaving out of our discussion?"

Alex suddenly remembered the metal talisman in his

pocket. "I don't know if this is anything or not, but I found it in the room right after Cliff was killed."

He handed the scored metal to her, and she flipped it over in her hand. "What is it?"

"I don't have a clue," Alex admitted. "I don't even know if it had anything to do with the display. It could have been there for weeks."

Elise handed it back to him and asked, "Where did you find it?"

"It was leaning against one of the baseboards near the floor grate," Alex said.

"Then it wasn't there before the emerald went on display," Elise said resolutely.

"How can you be so sure?" Alex asked.

"I cleaned every inch of that room, Alex, including the grates. Take my word for it, it wasn't there."

"Then I need to show it to the sheriff," Alex said. He knew what a meticulous worker Elise was.

But what did it mean?

He tucked the metal back into his pocket as he finished up the last of the room.

"Well, that takes care of my chores. Are you ready for lunch?" Alex asked her.

"That sounds great, but there's one thing I want to do first."

Alex laughed gently. "Let me guess. You'd like to check on Reston Shay."

Elise said, "You think you're so smart."

"But am I right?"

Elise frowned a second, then said, "I'll be able to enjoy my lunch more if I know he's okay."

"Then we'll go check on him right now. I don't want anything distracting you."

"From what?" Elise asked.

"The view, of course," Alex said with a slight smile, as they went off to Reston Shay's room to check on their eccentric guest.

7

Once again, there was no response when Alex and Elise knocked on the millionaire's door.

"Surely you don't think he's still asleep," Elise said.

Alex studied the closed door a second, then said, "I guess it's possible."

"Alex, I've got a bad feeling about this. Let's go in and check on him."

Elise's nervous state was getting to Alex. He decided the only way to settle it was to do as she asked and check on their guest. After all, there was no "Do Not Disturb" sign hanging from his door, one that was available to every room. Elise had come up with a new design, one with the lighthouse in the background, taken from one of Mor Pendleton's photographs he'd snapped during a photography class.

"Here goes nothing," Alex said as he knocked one last time before using his passkey. He felt the hairs on the back of his neck tingle as he pulled out the key and slid the door open.

He was in no mood to find another body at Hatteras West.

With a wave of relief, Alex saw that there was no sign of Reston Shay in the room. The bathroom door stood open and the shower curtain was pulled back. The bed hadn't been slept in, and only the hand soap had been freed from its wrapper.

"He's not here," Alex said.

"I can see that. But if he's not around the inn, where is he?"

Alex said, "He's not a captive here, Elise, Reston's free to come and go as he pleases."

Studying the untouched bed, Elise said, "He didn't sleep here."

"How can you be certain he didn't make up his own bed this morning before he left?"

She pointed to one corner of the bed as she lifted up the lighthouse quilt that covered it. "See this tuck? I'm the only one in the world who does it. Reston didn't stay here last night."

"So he decided to go home after all. There's nothing to worry about," Alex said.

"I have a bad feeling about this. Why would he pay for a room he wasn't going to sleep in? It doesn't make sense, Alex."

"If you're trying to figure Reston Shay out, you're going to need more than that to go on. Now why don't we have that lunch?"

Elise agreed, but Alex noticed that as he relocked Reston's room, Elise's gaze lingered there. Still, there was nothing he could do about the missing eccentric, at least not until after lunch.

The stairs of the lighthouse were too narrow for them to walk side by side, given the size of the picnic basket Elise had packed for their meal. Alex had hung the sign,

"Closed for One Hour" on the lighthouse's front doors and then locked them, something he did whenever he wanted to be alone at the top. Thankfully, there were no guests or townsfolk at the top when they got there, so he and Elise had the place to themselves.

"So where should we set up our picnic?" Alex asked.

Elise made a full circle around the top landing, gazing at the Blue Ridge Mountains on one side and the foothills laid out below the other. "Let's have lunch right here," she said. "That way I won't have to miss either view. Oh, Alex, it's glorious up here, isn't it?"

"It's my favorite place on earth," he said as he spread the blanket out.

As they ate, they pointed out different sights to each other, and though Alex had seen the views a million times, seeing them with Elise was always like looking through fresh eyes. He felt the tug of the mountains before him, watching with earnest amazement in the distance as clouds scudded by, as if brushing the tops of the trees.

He and Elise cleaned up when they were finished, stowing the paper plates and cups back in the basket and tying the trash up in a bag. Instead of heading back down the steps, Alex leaned on the railing and looked out. Elise joined him a few seconds later. She said, "I never get tired of this view."

Alex looked at her a second, then said, "Me either."

She laughed gently. "When I first saw your lighthouse, I couldn't imagine why anyone would build one in the mountains. Now I wonder why there aren't more."

"I've been saying that for years," Alex said. After a few more minutes, Elise said, "I hate to say this, but we'd better get back. We've got three loads of laundry, and the front desk is deserted."

Alex nodded, then spotted someone down below coming from the trees that separated the inn from Bear Rocks.

It was Patrick Thornton, and from the look of him, he was a real mess.

By the time Alex and Elise got down the steps, Patrick had just finished cleaning chunks of red clay from his boots near the front steps of the inn. There were splotches of clay along his denim jeans as well, most noticeably on his knees.

He looked apologetic as he said, "Surveyors manage to get into the most messes. I thought I'd come back for a clean change of clothes before I head into town. Is there a laundry there?"

Alex was about to direct him to the laundry-mat near Buck's Grill when Elise said, "We do laundry here as an added service for our guests."

"That's a relief," Patrick said. He stared at Elise for a few seconds, then asked, "Have we met?"

"I don't think so."

"My mistake. I'm afraid I've got a full load for you."

"No problem. Just leave it by your door and we'll see to it. Don't worry about the charge, we'll just add it to your bill when you check out."

"That would be great," Patrick said as he slipped past them in his stocking feet. Alex waited until he was gone to say, "Since when did we start taking in laundry? Is that a new service we're offering?"

"Any source of income we can tap, so much the better," Elise said.

"But there's more to it than that, isn't there?" Alex pushed.

Elise nodded. "Where did you tell me Thornton would be working this morning?"

Alex said, "He mentioned the orchard, and then Bear Rocks."

Elise nodded. "That's what I thought, but there's no mud at Bear Rocks, and the orchard is all grass under the trees. So how did your surveyor get so much clay on him?"

"Maybe he changed his plans," Alex said.

"Or maybe he's up to something," Elise countered.

"Oh, no, I'm rubbing off on you. Now I've got you jumping at shadows, too."

She shook her head. "I'm just more in tune with what's going on around me than I used to be. And yes, I do thank you for that. Now let's collect his clothes and see what we can uncover."

Alex laughed. "Why don't we at least wait until the poor man has a chance to shower and change clothes? We can spy on him later. Right now we need to tackle the sheets and towels."

Elise agreed, though Alex thought she was a bit reluctant to do so. Had he made her paranoid with his suspicions of their guests and the townsfolk of Elkton Falls? More likely, he had merely intensified that streak of curiosity within her.

As they did the sheets and towels, Alex saw that Elise's gaze kept returning to the clock, as if she was waiting for something. Thornton himself came into the laundry room just as Elise was ready to go collect his things. "Sorry there are so many," he said. "I appreciate you adding the laundry fees to my bill."

"It will be our pleasure," Elise said, taking the duffel bag from him.

After he was gone, she took the wet sheets out of one of the washers and threw them into a dryer. Instead of dumping all of his clothes into the machine after adding the detergent, Elise sorted each piece before putting it in, inspecting every stain and trace of soil carefully and riffling through the pockets.

After she was finished, Alex asked, "Find anything of interest?"

"He's certainly got a large collection of stains," she

said, "But other than that, there was nothing out of the ordinary, no notes in his pants pockets or clues in his shirt cuffs."

Alex said, "At least we made some extra money for the inn," but Elise didn't find anything amusing about it.

She said, "I want to go over his room again while he's gone."

"I already cleaned it, Elise. Believe me, there's nothing there."

She was about to reply when they both heard someone hailing them from the front desk. "Hello? Is anyone here? Hello?"

Alex and Elise walked back out front to find Fiona White, or as she preferred to be called, The Muffin Lady, waiting rather impatiently for them.

"I thought you'd both abandoned the inn. I was here an hour ago and no one was around then either."

"We were at lunch. Sorry, I forgot to put the sign up," Alex explained.

"No matter, it gave me the opportunity to explore your rock formation next door. What in the world is it called?"

"Bear Rocks," Alex said.

"Yes, I could quite see there was no vegetation growing there. Now what is the name?"

Alex said patiently, "Bear Rocks. That's B-E-A-R, as in Ursa."

"How quaint. I suppose bears used to frequent it in the winter?"

"Not that I'm aware of," Alex said, fighting to hide his smile. "One of the rocks looks like a black bear standing on its hind legs, and another forms a cradle, like a mother bear might."

"And no doubt there are baby bear boulders all around, as well." She dismissed their line of conversation with a wave of her hand. "Now let's get down to business. I trust my muffins have been doing well against the competition?"

Elise said cryptically, "It's too soon to tell."

The Muffin Lady said, "I can't imagine it's all that close a contest. Are you ready to place a standing order today?"

Alex was about to agree, Fiona's muffins were indeed a clear favorite over Sally Anne's, when Elise said, "We agreed on a one-week trial."

That generated another wave in the air from Fiona. "Mere formalities, but if you insist, I'll return at the end of the week, though I can't imagine Miss Sally Anne's offerings getting any takers when my muffins are available. It's a shame about her beau standing her up at the altar, isn't it?"

"It wasn't quite all that dramatic," Elise said, but Fiona didn't buy it.

"It sounded dramatic enough to me. And poor Irma Bean, ready to shut Mama Ravolini's down after this upstart comes to town."

"What have you heard?" Alex asked. Losing Mama Ravolini's, especially after the disastrous start at Monet's Garden, could be a real catastrophe for Elkton Falls.

"Just some idle chitchat I picked up around town," Fiona said as she started to walk away.

She was nearly out the door when Alex remembered that Fiona had visited the inn shortly before Cliff's murder and the theft. "Did you hear about what happened out here?"

She paused at the door, a crinkled frown on her brow. "What might that be?"

"The first time you visited us, a guard was murdered and a precious emerald was stolen from the inn."

She brushed it off with a curt shrug. "I concern myself with muffins. It's enough to keep me occupied, trust me. I don't know anything about your murder or your robbery."

After she was gone, as Elise and Alex returned to folding laundry, he said, "Do you have any interest in dinner tonight?"

"I don't know, Alex, two dinners out together two nights in a row? Besides, the Darcys are due in this evening, and I hate to be gone while a guest waits here for us."

"Relax, I'm not pressing you. I just thought we might get reservations at Irma's and see how she's doing."

Elise said, "You know, you're right, that's an excellent idea."

Alex added, "Should I invite Mor and Emma and make it a foursome again?"

Elise shook her head. "Why don't we let the newlyweds enjoy some time alone. I think dinner with just the two of us would be nice."

Alex had to agree. It would certainly have to be better than the last time they'd dined at Mama Ravolini's together alone. It had been the scene of their disastrous first date, and Alex was determined not to make the same mistakes again this time.

Visiting his old friend would just be an added bonus to the night. Alex left a note at the front desk in case the Darcys showed up, along with their room key. He'd work out the billing the next morning. It would be worth the added hassle, since it meant he'd be dining out with Elise. Besides, most guests seemed to expect the owner of a mountain lighthouse to be a little eccentric, and Alex hated to disappoint anybody.

Irma Bean's restaurant, given the name Mama Ravolini's because Irma had thought it sounded more authentic for her Italian fare, was emptier than Alex could ever remember seeing it. Irma hovered by the door, dressed in black as if she was in mourning, and as Alex and Elise came in, she looked grateful to have them dining with her.

"Hi, Irma, how are you?" Elise asked, gently touching the older woman's shoulder. Elise wore an understated print dress that highlighted her complexion, and if she had makeup on, it had been so skillfully applied that Alex couldn't see it. Still, something was different from her normal working appearance. Alex had foregone his suit and was wearing the shirt from L.L. Bean Elise had given him for his birthday and a pair of khaki Dockers. While it wasn't quite his suit, his clothes were definitely a step up from his normal day-to-day wardrobe.

Irma squeezed Elise's hand. "I'm holding my own," she said, but the fire was gone from her voice and her eyes. She waved at the tables and said, "Take your pick, there are plenty of choices tonight."

Irma handed Alex two menus and turned back to stare worriedly at the front door. As they found a table, Alex said, "I've never seen her like this before."

Elise looked around the room. "I'll bet you've never seen this place as deserted as it is tonight, either. I don't understand it. The prices alone should be enough to keep folks away from Monet's Garden. I can't imagine anyone going back who ate there last night."

"The novelty will wear off soon enough," Alex said, hoping it was true. While he enjoyed having Elise mostly to himself, he would have rather been surrounded by a roomful of other diners for Irma's sake. They had just placed their orders when one of their guests from the inn stopped by their table. Melva Flump was a walking fashion disaster, mixing stripes, checks, and plaids in her clothes with reckless abandon. Though she was about Alex's age, he couldn't imagine having anything else in common with the dour woman.

"Mr. Winston, Ms. Danton, I didn't realize you two were involved in a personal relationship."

Alex looked on in shock at Melva Flump as Elise said,

"We all have to eat, don't we, Ms. Flump? I hope you enjoy the rest of your evening."

She took the dismissal as it was intended, offered a curt, "Good night, then," and headed out of the restaurant, most likely on her way back to Hatteras West.

"No doubt we'll be the subject of tonight's postcard barrage," Elise said after she was gone.

"I can't wait to read the current installment," Alex agreed. Melva, though she didn't look it, was a most imaginative writer. Her prose was in the form of a chain of postcards, written in careful, spidery print each night, one after the other until her tale was told, all addressed to a woman named Kim in Queens and neatly numbered just below the stamp to insure the proper sequence of reading. The cards' fronts were identical, they were the lighthouse postcards Alex offered free to his guests at the inn, but the writing squeezed into the small squares on the back was anything but common. Two nights ago, Alex had read with surprise as Melva relived a brief encounter with Patrick Thornton in most graphic detail. Alex knew this was pure fiction, as he'd witnessed Thornton picking up a pair of books Melva had dropped in the hallway before offering her a brief goodnight. Not so in Melva's mind. She'd invited him back to her room, and one thing led to another, all in detail that made Alex blush. Elise had caught him reading them, chided him for being so nosy, then picked up the missives just as quickly as Alex finished each entry. Alex had justified reading them to her, arguing that if she'd wanted privacy, she would have written sealed letters instead of postcards. He couldn't imagine what Melva's friend must think of the Hatteras West Inn; some kind of Southern Club Med most likely.

It had become part of their evening ritual to see just where Melva's imagination would be taking her later that night.

As they waited for their meal, Alex studied some of the

closest photographs of the near-famous hanging from the walls. He was sitting close to Yardley Hink's snapshot, a big grin plastered on the insurance salesman's face. Yardley's claim to fame was a brief stint on *Who Wants to Be Rich*, a cable television show that offered a top prize of ten thousand dollars to the winner. Yardley had failed to guess the fifty-dollar question correctly after staying up too late the night before taking in the sights of Atlanta; at least that had been his excuse. Though his appearance had lasted less than thirty seconds, apparently it had been enough to gain him a spot on the wall. Alex wondered if he'd ever manage anything deemed noteworthy enough to be included in the gallery, then wondered if he'd allow it, knowing how much fun he had with some of the rogues on display there.

Elise pulled him from his thoughts and asked, "So what are we going to do?"

"About Melva? She's harmless, I wouldn't worry about her."

Elise shook her head. "I'm talking about finding the murderer. It's got to be someone right in front of us, but I don't have a clue where to start."

Alex touched Elise's hand briefly, then asked, "Could we not talk about Cliff's murder and the theft tonight? Why don't we leave Hatteras West where it is and enjoy our meal?"

"Alex Winston, are you under the impression this really is a date?"

Alex nodded slightly. "Call me hopeless, but I think there's still a chance for us."

Elise studied him longer than he was comfortable with, then said, "You know, it's possible you just might be right."

Their moment was interrupted by a booming voice from the front of the restaurant. Elise said, "It appears that great minds think alike."

Alex didn't have to look up to know that his best friend, Mor Pendleton, was there, with his wife no doubt beside him.

Alex stood up as they approached. "Hey, you two."

Emma smiled their way, then tugged at Mor's arm. "Let's give them some privacy, you big goon."

He ignored the tug. "They were getting ready to invite us to sit down, so why not save them the breath."

"Mor Pendleton, I swear, sometimes you can be so thick. If they'd wanted us to join them, they would have called and invited us out in the first place."

Elise said, "We thought you two might enjoy some time alone yourselves."

Mor said, "Nonsense, there's always room in our lives for our friends."

Emma shook her head sadly. "I thought he could be trained, but I'm beginning to have my doubts."

Alex said, "He's just going to take more work than you figured on."

Mor said, "Hey, I'm standing right here. So what's it going to be, should we find another table and pretend we didn't see you?"

Alex was ready to suggest just that when Elise said, "Nonsense, we'd be delighted to have you join us."

So much for their date, Alex thought as the couple took seats across from them.

He'd been close, but close didn't count.

At least not in the dating game he and Elise were playing.

8

Halfway through their meal, much better than their offerings the night before, Sheriff Armstrong walked into Mama Ravolini's and took one of the singles' tables against the wall. Alex loved the fact that Irma Bean recognized that some folks dined alone and didn't like being treated like pariahs. He'd taken advantage of the discrete tables himself a time or two in the past.

Elise said, "Alex, here's your chance. Did you bring it with you?"

"What's that?"

"That odd piece of metal you found," Elise explained.

Alex tapped the breast pocket of his shirt. "I've got it right here, but it can wait, can't it?"

"He needs to see it now," Elise said.

"Hey, what's all the whispering about?" Mor asked.

Emma nudged his elbow. "Now you just hush, Mor Pendleton. I knew we should have given them some privacy."

Alex said, "No, we're thrilled to have you. I just need to speak with the sheriff for a second."

Mor said, "No doubt Elise can fill us in while you're gone."

She looked to Alex, waiting for his approval to share the information, and after thinking about it a second, Alex nodded his agreement. After all, there were no secrets between the four of them. Mor and Emma had lent a hand in some of their impromptu investigations in the past.

Alex walked over to Armstrong and was surprised to find a salad already in front of the man.

"Wow, that's fast service," Alex said.

"I get the same thing every night," Armstrong grumbled. "A salad and a small plate of spaghetti."

"How's the diet working out?" Alex asked.

"I've lost three pounds," Armstrong admitted grudgingly. "Not sure if it's worth it, though." He started to take a bite, then put his fork back down. "Is there anything else I can do for you, Alex?"

"I found something out at the inn I thought you needed to see," Alex admitted, pulling the piece of metal from his pocket. "What do you make of that?"

"Where was it?" Armstrong asked as he took the metal from Alex.

"It was in the room where Cliff was murdered, and Elise swears it wasn't there before the exhibition."

Armstrong held the piece up to the flickering candle at his table, studied it a second, then handed it back to Alex. "I can't imagine it being important. Somebody on the tour must have dropped it. Probably some kid."

"So you don't want it?" Alex asked.

"Nope, feel free to put it in your Lost and Found, if it makes you feel better."

Armstrong's explanation was perfectly reasonable, and Alex felt embarrassed when he realized his overactive imagination had most likely been at work again.

As he tucked the metal piece back into his pocket, Alex asked, "Are you making any progress in the case?"

Armstrong looked around before he spoke. "This is strictly between us, but I don't have a thing to go on. It's driving me crazy."

"No leads at all?"

Armstrong shrugged. "I'm trying to track down Cliff's ex-wife, and I've got the state boys looking into the stolen gem market. They've got contacts way out of my league, but so far, there hasn't been a whisper about the emerald. There were no prints on the letter opener, so that was a wash, too."

"How about in the room itself?" Alex asked.

"You're kidding, right? Most of Elkton Falls passed through that room, and a ton of strangers we'll never be able to identify. I told Irene not to waste her time."

"So somebody's going to get away with murder," Alex said bluntly.

"Now I didn't say that," Armstrong grumbled. "These things take time, you know that, Alex." He looked at the lean salad and bare drizzle of dressing, then added, "Listen, I'm on the clock, so I need to get to this."

"Sorry to interrupt you, Sheriff. Enjoy your meal," Alex said as he headed back to the table.

Elise asked, "So what did he say? Did he think it was a clue?"

"Just that I was probably losing my mind," Alex said. When he explained Armstrong's theory about the metal piece, Mor said, "You know, I hate to admit it, but old Strong Arms is probably right."

"I don't know," Elise said with some hesitation.

Emma said, "Why don't we forget about it tonight and just have a nice meal? Irma's outdone herself, hasn't she?"

Mor said, "I second that motion."

Later, after they were finished with their meals, Mor pushed his empty plate toward the center of the table and said, "That ravioli was so good I think I'll have another order."

He was flagging their waiter down when Emma said, "Mor Pendleton, don't you think you've had enough? Honestly, two plates of food in one sitting?"

He grinned at his bride. "Emma, I've been known to eat three helpings when the mood strikes me. You know that. It's not like I've never done it before."

"You're going to get chubby," she said.

"I don't think so, but if I do, that means there will be more of me to love."

Emma said, "Now that you have a wife, you need to take better care of yourself."

"Yes, Mom, I promise," Mor said with a grin.

Emma started to explode, Alex could see it in the flash in her eyes, then she took a deep breath, and instead of arguing, let out a long, healthy laugh.

Elise asked, "Are you all right?"

Emma wiped the tears from the corners of her eyes and said, "I am now." She turned to her husband and said, "I've been dreadful lately, haven't I?"

"Just since the honeymoon," Mor said.

"Okay, I deserved that. No more bossing, no more mothering. You're a big boy, Mor Pendleton. I know in my heart you managed fine on your own without me all these years. I'll try to do better."

Mor, obviously touched by her declaration, said, "And I'll try not to give you so much grief." He squeezed his bride's hand and said, "Hey, this marriage deal has a pretty steep learning curve, doesn't it?"

Emma bussed him with a kiss, then said, "Don't worry, you're starting to get the hang of it."

The waiter approached and asked if he could help them.

Mor said, "We'll take the check, whenever you're ready."

Emma said, "Oh, have your ravioli, I don't mind."

Mor admitted sheepishly, "To be honest with you, I ate

so much rich stuff on that cruise, I could stand to skip an extra serving now and then."

When the waiter came back, Alex fully expected there to be two checks. Instead, he slid a single bill in front of Mor. Alex reached for his wallet and asked, "Should we split it ourselves or have him make out another check?"

Mor said, "Nonsense, my friend, dinner is on us."

Alex said, "Thanks for the offer, but I've got ours."

Emma said, "Please, Alex, let us treat. You two have done so much for us. It would be our pleasure."

Alex was about to extend his protest when Elise reached across the table and squeezed his hand. As she did so, she said, "Thank you so much. It was wonderful."

Alex added grudgingly, "At least let me get the tip."

Mor started to reply when Emma spoke up. "That would be fine." Then she looked at Elise and said, "You know what? They may both be trainable, at that."

Elise's laughter was as gentle as the breeze. "Let's hope so."

Mor pulled out his credit card, handed it to the waiter, then said to Alex, "I don't know about you, buddy, but I think I'm insulted."

"Hey, at least they didn't say we were both hopeless."

"I guess that's something," Mor admitted.

Irma hugged them all as they left, and Alex was happy to see that the place was starting to fill up. Word of Monet's prices must have been burning up the kudzu gossip vine. Irma had a flush to her cheeks that hadn't been there before as she saw the prodigals returning in such force.

Outside, it was starting to rain, and the two couples went their separate ways. Alex held Elise's door open for her and then climbed into the driver's side of his aging, gray Ford pickup truck just before the deluge hit. It was tense driving back to the inn in the storm, and Elise sat there quietly, watching the road right along with him. What normally took fifteen minutes to drive took them nearly forty-five, and by the time they pulled up Point Road, Alex could feel the muscles in his back strained from the intensity of his vigil.

As the rain drummed down on the roof of the truck, Alex said, "I didn't even bring an umbrella. We're going to get soaked."

Elise said, "We could sit out here and wait it out."

"That sounds good to me."

Elise looked at the lighthouse, then said, "We should turn on the lens. Nobody would complain in the storm."

"Don't bet on it. I'm already in the doghouse about last time."

"I thought Tracy was going to do something to help you."

Alex said, "She's been trying, but there's so much she wants to get accomplished, and the town council's been giving her grief every step of the way."

"That honeymoon didn't last long," Elise said.

"I wasn't expecting it to," Alex replied. "I told her to take it easy at first, but Tracy has big plans for Elkton Falls. She wants to restore the town to all its former glory."

"She'll be good for the place," Elise said. There was a noticeable break in the rain, and she added, "Should we run for it?"

"I'm game if you are."

They broke free of the truck and dashed to the front porch before another wave of rain came down. "Wow, that's a real soaking rain," Elise said.

"It will take more than that to touch our drought. We're still twelve inches short for the year."

They went inside the Main Keeper's Quarters and found someone had taken the initiative to light the fire in the lobby's fireplace.

"I'm going to go change," Elise said. "I'll be right back."

Alex was comfortable enough in his outfit, so he checked the answering machine for messages, something he did routinely whenever he was away from the inn.

There was a blinking "2," and Alex hit replay. The first message was from Reston Shay. "Listen, I had something I had to take care of last night in Charlotte. This guy with the insurance company is driving me crazy. Help him settle this fast if there's anything you can do, will you? I still want the room, don't rent it out. My assistant will bring a check by in the morning; I want to reserve it for the next month. One condition though. I don't want anyone going in the room. That means you and Elise, too. The insurance guy insisted. Talk to you later."

The second message was from Monet, the restaurant owner. "Mr. Winston, I need to speak with you at your earliest convenience. Perhaps you can drop by this evening. I await your reply." As an afterthought, he added, "This is Monet from the—," as the machine cut him off.

He was stoking the fire when Elise rejoined him, wearing a flannel shirt and jeans, her outfit of choice, and truth be told, Alex's favorite. When she was dressed elegantly, he felt awkward with her, knowing full well how striking she really was. In jeans though, he could see her more for what she was, a friend and coworker with a good heart and a strong spirit, and not just a lovely woman.

Elise started to sit by the fire, then said, "Hang on, I'll be right back."

"He's not here," Alex said.

"Who's not here?"

"Reston Shay. He isn't in his room."

Elise said, "How did you know that was where I was going?"

"Call it a hunch."

She said, "But you're worried too, aren't you?"

"Why do you say that?"

"You checked on him yourself."

Alex hit replay on the answering machine, and Elise listened to both messages. After Monet was finished, she said, "How odd."

"Monet is a rule unto himself, isn't he?"

Elise shook her head. "That's not what I'm talking about. Why would Reston take the room for an entire month when he has a home not ten minutes from here? I don't buy his story that it's so it will be available to the insurance investigator. There's got to be more to it than that."

Alex said, "I told you before, he's a real eccentric. Just think of it as a guaranteed month's stay. We could use it."

She said, "I know, but it's still odd."

Alex laughed. "We never seem to have a shortage of that around Hatteras West."

They were just settled in by the fire when the front door of the inn banged open. Patrick Thornton walked in, knocking the rain from the brim of his hat and hanging his jacket up by the door. "It's still coming down out there," the surveyor said.

"We're in for a good storm," Alex agreed.

Thornton ran a hand through his hair, then looked intently at Elise before speaking. "Excuse me, I'm sure this must sound like some kind of line, but are you sure we haven't met before?"

"I don't believe so."

He shook his head. "Your face is awfully familiar."

Elise said, "I'm sorry, I don't remember you."

"I've got it. Didn't I see you in the Miss West Virginia pageant a few years ago?"

"No, it must have been someone else."

"Sorry, my mistake. My cousin was entered, and I could swear . . . oh, well, I'll say good night. I've got a big day ahead of me tomorrow, and slogging through the mud won't make my work any easier."

"Where will you be tomorrow?" Alex asked.

"I haven't decided yet, but it will be wet, I'll tell you that."

After he was gone, Elise was brooding about something. Alex asked, "What's wrong?"

"It's nothing."

He persisted. "I've seen that look before, something's troubling you. If you want to talk about it, I'd be happy to listen."

"That pageant nonsense," Elise said.

"Don't hold that against him. Anybody could make a mistake," Alex said.

Elise studied her thumb a few seconds, then said, "He was right. It was me."

"I thought you gave up pageants long before that." Elise had shared part of her history with Alex before, but only in vague terms.

"I needed the scholarship to finish college, and Mom and Dad were going through a rough time at the inn. I got it, too. I was first runner-up." She said the last as if she was admitting she'd been arrested.

"I can't believe it," Alex said.

"That I'd enter a beauty pageant, knowing the way I felt about them?"

"No, that you didn't win," Alex said, his disbelief an honest reaction.

"Please, Alex, there are millions of pretty women in the world."

"So why did you deny it when Thornton asked you about it?"

"Because I entered for all the wrong reasons. I'm not slamming the women who choose to participate, but for me it was a travesty. Here I'd battled with my mother about all of the junior pageants she'd forced me into entering, and I was going after the biggest prize of them all. I'm not proud of it."

"Did you cheat to get first runner-up? Steal somebody's sheet music or trip another contestant?" Alex asked softly.

"What? Of course not."

"So why apologize? You stayed in school and got your degree. Wasn't that what it was really about?"

Elise sighed, then said, "My whole life I've been saddled with this genetic windfall, and the entire time, I've been trying to prove myself in spite of it. So what did I do when things got dicey? I caved in."

"Don't be so hard on yourself." He stared at the flames a few moments, then asked, "So what was your talent?"

"No, sir, you're not getting that out of me. That is all ancient history."

Alex grinned. "I would have voted for you."

She ruffled his hair as she got up. "I know you would have. Good night, Alex."

"Good night."

After she was gone, Alex lingered over the fire, reveling in the feeling of security that being in the inn gave him. Outside, the storm was lashing at the windows, pounding down the rain, and inside, he was dry and warm and safe from its reaches. The front door banged open in the wind, and a couple struggled in with their suitcases.

"You must be the Darcys, Vince and Laura."

The man shook the rain off his jacket and said, "What are you, some kind of mind reader?"

"Don't give me that much credit. I've been expecting you."

The man's wife said, "Sorry to keep you up. We ran into some problems with the map."

Vince said, "Now let's not get started with that again, Laura."

Alex checked them in swiftly and showed them to their room. By the time he got back to the lobby, the fire was dying, but he promised himself to enjoy the last remnants of it while he could.

All was well with the world, until an explosion on the second floor jolted him out of his seat and sent him racing up the stairs.

9

Elise joined him as he passed her door. The sound had come from one of the second floor guest rooms, and Alex couldn't imagine what could have caused it. It had sounded like something between a gunshot and a mortar shell going off.

He found Claudia Post, one of their guests who'd been with them six days, standing in the hallway outside her room covered with a purple concoction from the curlers in her hair to the pink fuzzy slippers on her feet. The flannel nightgown she was wearing would never be the same. Claudia looked nothing like the reserved, older woman who walked the grounds of the property every day. The smell hovering around her was like rotten grapes left out in the hot sun.

"What happened?" Alex asked as he surveyed the dripping purple puddles on the hardwood floors. He hoped whatever it was wouldn't leave a permanent stain on the floor, now that he'd seen that his guest was unhurt.

"What did you say?" Claudia asked, driving her fingertips into her ears.

"Are you all right?"

She smiled sheepishly. "No fight. Just a little accident."

Elise went to the linen closet in the hallway and grabbed a handful of fresh towels. He noticed as she casually dropped one at Claudia's feet, sopping up the liquid before it could stain the floor.

Alex still didn't have a clue about what had happened when Claudia said, "I brought some homemade wine with me. It appears I may have used a tad too much sugar in the fermentation process for that particular batch." She bit her lower lip, then added loudly, "The bathroom's a mess, I'm afraid. I'll be willing to cover whatever additional charges there are for cleaning it, above and beyond my bill."

Alex cringed at the thought of the cleanup job ahead of them. "Let's worry about that later. Right now, we need to get you some clean clothes."

"Yes, a little did get up my nose, but I'll be fine." The explosion had deafened the woman, or at least lessened her hearing for the moment.

Elise said, "Let's move you to another room so we can get you right in the tub."

"I don't need a backrub," Claudia said. "I said I'll be fine."

Elise steered their guest down the hall to another room as she turned to Alex and said, "Grab her things, would you?"

They settled Claudia in the room next door, then went about the arduous cleaning process. There was wine everywhere in the bathroom, from the ceiling to the baseboard, covering nearly every square inch of space, from wall to porcelain to cast iron.

"It's not coming off the walls," Elise said.

Alex surveyed the room, then said, "You know, this bathroom might look nice painted purple."

"We'll have to paint it, but I don't think purple's the

right choice. What on earth was she thinking? At least she opened it in here and not in the room."

Alex paled at the thought of something happening to the quilt his mother had made, now covering the bed. Since the fire, they'd lost several of the handmade quilts, and Alex now loaned them out grudgingly to their guests. Claudia had appeared safe enough, but that was clearly not the case. He thought about pulling them out of circulation in the rooms altogether, but making the beds every day, smoothing the quilts out, brought back memories of his mother; the touch of her hand on his brow, the way she sang as she worked, the hint of jasmine she always wore. Those quilts had been created to give comfort. They didn't belong stored away in some closet.

Elise saw him stroke the quilt gently. "That could have been much worse," she said. "We really should protect your mother's quilts."

"We can't put them up, they belong out where people can see them."

Elise said, "I have an idea. Why don't we frame them and hang them in each room? They're much too special to take any more chances."

"I want people to be able to enjoy them," Alex said.

"All the more reason to preserve them before they're ruined. We've lost more than one since I've been here, and I'd hate to see them all disappear."

Alex studied the quilt again, remembering. "Maybe you're right."

"I'll talk to Mor about framing them," she said.

"I can do it myself. He'll think I've flipped my lid."

Elise said, "Not if I tell him it was my idea. I know you're a fine woodworker, but you don't have enough time for it anymore."

Alex shook his head. "That's true enough, but go ahead and let him think I'm crazy. I don't mind taking the blame. It will give him something to rib me about."

"Alex, do you think they're happy?"

"Emma and Mor? I'd have to say so. Why do you ask?"

She bit her lip. "They seem to fuss at each other quite a bit, don't they?"

"They always have. I never believed for one second their marriage vows would change that. You've got two strong personalities there, Elise; they're bound to clash sometimes. Don't forget, Emma already suffered through one bad marriage, and Mor's never been married at all. I can't imagine the adjustment process those two are going through." When he saw that his words weren't comforting her, he said, "Don't worry, I'm sure they'll be fine."

By the time they finished cleaning the room it was just before midnight. There was still the distinct aroma of spoiled grape juice in the air, though Elise had opened the windows the second they'd started cleaning. She said, "I'm afraid this room will be out of commission until we can get rid of that smell."

"That's odd," Alex said as he pushed the cleaning cart out into the hallway.

"What?" Elise asked.

"That explosion brought us both running, but neither of our other guests on this floor even peeked out their doors." There was no way Thornton or Melva could have slept through the commotion.

"Not everyone keeps innkeepers' hours, Alex. Maybe they're both still out."

Alex smiled. "Together? Could Melva's postcards have more than a ring of truth in them?"

Elise said, "After what I've seen tonight, anything's possible." She glanced at the clock in the hallway and said, "Six A.M. is going to come awfully early tomorrow. Good night, Alex."

"See you tomorrow. Today, I mean," Alex said as the clock ticked past midnight.

Alex was exhausted, but there was no way he could go

to bed before he took another shower. Even after scrubbing his skin raw, there was a lingering aroma of grape juice on him. He couldn't imagine what Claudia must smell like.

Finally, it was the last day of the great muffin trials, and Alex knew there was hardly any point in continuing the contest. The Muffin Lady's offerings were all taken by the end of breakfast, while Sally Anne's were mostly untouched. Alex was not looking forward to telling Buck and his daughter that, beginning next week, they'd be going with a different supplier. He'd have to find a way to break the news to them with the minimum amount of acrimony. After all, they were his friends, first and foremost, and friendship was very important to Alex. After he and Elise set up their morning breakfast offerings, Alex checked the answering machine as was part of his morning routine. It was as much a habit for him as walking out to the mailbox at the end of Point Road to collect the day's mail.

There was a "1" on the machine, and Alex hit replay as Elise grabbed a cup of coffee.

"Alex, again, please call me when you get in. This is Monet." The number to the restaurant followed, then the time was given. Monet had called twenty minutes after he'd gone to bed. What could have possibly been so urgent that it required a conversation in the middle of the night? In the middle of *Alex's* night, he remembered. Surely the restaurateur kept different hours than he did as an innkeeper. It must have been hard keeping in sync with the rest of the world when Monet worked such off hours.

Elise joined him and asked, "Who was the message from?"

"Mr. Monet. He's called twice, but I haven't had the chance to return his calls. We're on completely different time schedules."

Elise took a bite of one of the jumbo strawberry muffins and said, "I wonder what he wants?"

"I'll find out today, I promise."

As their guests came down for breakfast, Alex kept a mental list on who left the inn and who went back to their rooms. Patrick Thornton, dressed for the outdoors again, stopped at the desk on his way out.

"Alex, I'm going to be staying longer than I'd originally anticipated. Is that a problem?"

Since there was a dearth of guests, Alex had no problem with that at all. He pretended to study his reservation list, shook his head a few times, then said, "I think I can fit you in. Any idea how long you'll be with us?"

"Sorry, I don't have a clue."

"We'll try to keep something open, then."

"Thanks."

Alex said, "I hope it goes smoothly for you."

The surveyor nodded. "So do I."

After he was gone, Alex said, "I'm going to get a jump on my rooms. Can you handle the cleanup here?"

"No problem. When you're finished, come find me. I want to go with you when you talk to Monet. I've got the feeling something is wrong."

He promised, then went to Patrick Thornton's room to start his day of cleaning.

The room was as neat as he'd left it, and Alex wondered yet again about the guests who made their own beds. He had one woman from Virginia who brought her own cleaning supplies with her for the annual week she spent at the inn. Earline Christine claimed that cleaning calmed her, and Alex had promised her a go at the glass at the top of the lighthouse on her next visit.

Alex did a perfunctory check of the bathroom and noticed that the toilet was still running. Sometimes the chains got hung up and Alex lifted the lid to straighten it.

The cause of the problem was immediately obvious, but Alex didn't know what to do about it.

He went back to the lobby and found Elise. "That was quick," she said.

"I need you," Alex said simply, and she followed him to Patrick Thornton's room without a single question. That was one of the things he liked about her. Elise knew when it was time for discretion; there were things the inn's guests didn't need to know about that were going on at Hatteras West.

After he shut the door to Thornton's room, Elise asked, "What is it?"

"Come into the bathroom."

She followed him in, and Alex gestured to the open toilet tank. Elise looked inside at the carefully bundled package about the size and shape of a large flashlight, then said, "What do you think it is, drugs?"

"I don't know. The question is, what do we do about it?"

Elise asked, "How did you find it? I do a thorough job of cleaning, but even I'm not that meticulous."

"The toilet was running, so I looked in to see if I could fix it." Alex nudged the tube slightly, freeing the chain and dropping the stopper. The water started to fill again immediately.

"Should we call Armstrong?" Elise asked.

"And tell him what? Elise, I'm not sure what he could do about this. We don't *know* Thornton's up to anything."

Elise said, "He's not hiding his toothbrush in there."

"So do you think we should open it?"

She studied the wrapping, then reached down and pulled the bundle out. Grabbing a hand towel, Elise dried off the plastic and duct tape. "I don't know how we could rewrap this without him knowing we found it."

"Let me see it," Alex said as he accepted the package. It was surprisingly heavy for its size. "It feels like it's full of lead," Alex said as he hefted it up and down. "One thing's certain, I don't think it's drugs. Or else why would it be so heavy?"

Elise said, "The weight might just be to keep it from floating to the top of the tank. So what do you think we should do about it?"

"Let's put it back for now. I need to think about this." He started to slide the package back in the reservoir tank, then flushed the toilet to drain the water temporarily. Placing the tube on the bottom of the tank, Alex watched as the water refilled.

"I don't like this," Elise said.

"Neither do I, but what can we do about it?"

"We can watch him," she said. "I wonder," she added, staring at the tube.

"What?"

"Could it be holding Reston Shay's emerald?"

Alex shook his head. "Not unless he cut it up. I doubt the Carolina Rhapsody would fit inside it."

"I suppose you're right. So he might not have stolen the gem but, he's still up to something."

Alex left the bathroom and deadbolted the main door to the room. "Why don't we have a quick look around while he's gone?"

Elise smiled. "You're on."

They went through the room thoroughly, and were both surprised by the lack of personal items Patrick Thornton had brought with him to Hatteras West. There were stacks of charts and maps on the table, covered with cryptic marks and symbols that Alex didn't recognize. Other than that, it was hard to believe the man was even using his room at the inn.

"Nothing," Elise said. "I don't get it, but I'm not giving up on him."

"I'd be stunned if you did," Alex replied. "Let's both think about this, and we can discuss it later."

She agreed, and left to clean the guestrooms in the other

building. Alex had been tempted to cut the package open
and see what Thornton was hiding, but he couldn't bring
himself to violate his guest's privacy without more of a
reason than just to satisfy his curiosity.

After replacing the dirty towels with fresh ones, Alex
reluctantly left Thornton's room and started on the next
one on his list.

Alex was finished with his rooms and decided to
start working on the mail at the front desk in the lobby of
Main. Two of his guests, Melva Flump and Laura Darcy,
were playing a game of backgammon, while Morgan Raye,
a professor from Carolina visiting on sabbatical, dozed by
the fireplace, a book tented neatly on his chest. Morgan
had been in that spot for the past three days, getting up
only for meals and other such essential breaks. He'd gone
through a remarkably small amount of reading material,
but the man had taken a most prestigious amount of naps.
Alex envied him the rest, and could see himself taking exactly that kind of vacation if he could ever afford to take
time off from his inn. Among the bills and reservation re-
quests, there was a letter in the pile from Harry Pickering,
a friend he sometimes corresponded with who was another
lighthouse innkeeper living on the North Carolina Outer
Banks twenty miles from the original Cape Hatteras Lighthouse. The two had been exchanging letters for years, living in the same state but separated by the miles from
mountain to coast. They'd even managed to meet when
Harry had been in Greensboro visiting his wife's family.
The two men, sharing so much, had gotten along from the
start.

Alex skimmed the letter, wondering what Harry was up
to, and nearly dropped it when he read the opening.

*Alex, my friend, I've got a wild idea, and I'm not
sure how you're going to feel about it, but hear me*

*out before you say no. Barbara has been talking
about a vacation to the mountains for so long my
ears are bleeding, but you know, more than anyone
else, how precarious a living this innkeeping life is.
Still, a vacation is long past due for us, as I'm sure
it is for you. So here's my crazy idea. Why don't we
swap inns for a couple of weeks when things slow
down in the winter season? I remember you telling
me how much you could use a break yourself. You
could run Cape Kidd, and Barbara and I could take
care of Hatteras West. Who better to watch over our
lighthouse inns than each other! Think about it, and
if it sounds like something you'd like to do, call me
and we'll work out the details. You and Elise should
have plenty of time to explore the coastline while
you're here, and Barbara and I could take a few day-
trips to Boone and Blowing Rock. She's been aching
to dig for emeralds in Hiddenite too.*

*Let me know what you think. If it sounds too crazy
for you, don't sweat it, I promise I won't be offended.*

More later, from one lighthouse nut to another,
Your friend,
Harry

Alex looked up to see Elise standing nearby. "What is
it?" she asked. "Bad news?"

"Harry Pickering wants to trade inns with us this winter. It's crazy, but he's invited us to run Cape Kidd while
he and Barbara take over Hatteras West."

Elise said, "Are we going to do it?"

"Do you mean to tell me you're interested?" Alex
asked.

She said, "You know I've never been to the Outer
Banks. I've been dying to see the Cape Hatteras Lighthouse."

"Just look out the window," Alex said.

"You know what I mean. We could eat seafood every night."

Alex admitted, "I'm allergic."

"Oh, that's right, I forgot. Still, there are walks on the beach, we could hunt for seashells, and best of all, there are lighthouses out there I haven't seen yet."

"So you're willing to take a busman's holiday and do this?"

Elise said, "It's your inn, Alex, so it's got to be your decision."

"But what do you really think?"

Elise said, "I think it could be wonderful."

"You know, it might be fun at that," Alex said as he tapped the letter on the counter. It could be just what he needed, running another lighthouse inn in a different part of North Carolina. And maybe getting Elise in such romantic surroundings would give her the nudge he'd been hoping for. A walk along the beach in moonlight could lead to a new level in the relationship.

Alex was about to agree when Mr. Monet, the restaurateur, walked in looking quite agitated about something. Only then did Alex realize he'd neglected to call the man back.

10

"Mr. Winston, do you have a moment?"

Alex nodded. "Certainly. I apologize for not returning your telephone calls, but things have been busy here."

Monet waved a hand in the air. "No excuses necessary, sir. I've been meaning to visit you long before we first met. I'm well acquainted with the travails of running an inn."

"Have you done it yourself?" Alex asked.

"Me? No sir, but I was, for a time, in the employ of a rather large hotel restaurant, and the manager befriended me. I know the headaches you must have."

"So what's on your mind?" Alex asked.

Monet looked around, noticed the people in the lobby, and asked, "Is there somewhere private we could speak?"

"My office isn't much, but at least it has a door that closes," Alex said lightly.

"It will be fine," Monet said. He turned to Elise and said, "If you'll excuse us?"

"Certainly," she said. "I've got work to do myself."

After they were safely ensconced in Alex's tiny office,

Monet said, "I've been quite troubled by something. You and your friends haven't returned to my restaurant."

Alex looked at his hands. "It's only been a few days."

Monet said, "I know sometimes I push too hard, but I thought that after our conversation the other night you might be the one to help me." Monet's mustache started to tremble, and it looked as if the man was about to cry. He bit back the emotion, then continued. "Forgive me for coming here and burdening you with my problems."

Monet started to get up when Alex said, "There's nothing to forgive. If you need a friendly ear, I'm right here."

"It is too much to ask," Monet said.

Alex said, "Nonsense. Everybody needs to unload now and then. If I can help, I will."

Monet slumped back into his chair. "There is no one else I can unburden myself to, no one I can call a true friend. I'm afraid I've made a dreadful mistake."

Alex listened, waiting for Monet to go on, afraid that if he said anything, did anything but nod and look sympathetic, Monet would bolt. And the man had something on his mind, troubles he needed to share.

After a few moments, Monet continued. "Everything I have, everything I am, is invested in my restaurant. It is my dream, at last come true, but it's quickly turning into a nightmare. My chef quitting was only one in a long line of difficulties."

"Have you replaced him yet?"

Monet nodded. "The new man is quite good, but my customers are not coming back. Why is that, do you know?"

Alex took a deep breath, then said, "Would you really like to know what I think, or are you looking for sympathy?"

"I need the truth," Monet said, "no matter how bitter it is to take."

Alex said, "Okay, but remember, you asked. Your prices

are way too high for Elkton Falls and the menu is a little too rich. But I'm not the one you should be asking."

Again Monet started to get up when Alex continued. "There are two women you should be talking to, and one of them is right here."

"You have a guest who is a restaurateur?"

Alex said, "I can do one better than that. My housekeeper, Elise Danton, has a degree in hotel/motel management, and experience, as well. She might be able to give you some insights that will help."

"And the second woman?" Monet asked.

"Irma Bean."

"Mama Ravolini herself? Surely you jest, I am her competitor. Why should she help me?"

"Don't sell Irma short. She's a good woman with a big heart. She might just surprise you. Think about it. What's the worst thing that could happen, she refuses to help you?"

"No, Alex, the worst thing is that I could lose my dream."

"So fight for it and try to fix what's not working for you. Hang on, I'll be right back." Alex found Elise in the lobby preparing to dust. "How'd you like to trade?"

"Is Mr. Monet still here?"

"He's in my office," Alex said, "and he needs your advice about running a restaurant in Elkton Falls."

"He should talk to Irma," Elise said.

"That's what I just told him, but I thought you could help him, too. You've been in the service business a long time."

"I'm not sure what I can do, but I'll try," she said as she handed him the dust rag and spray.

As Alex worked around the lobby dusting some of the collection of lighthouse paraphernalia and mountain culture his family had amassed, one of his guests came in the front door. Claudia Post had been out for her daily walk, something she'd done every chance she'd gotten since coming to the inn.

"Did you have a nice walk?" Alex asked. He made it a point to avoid any reference to the exploding wine incident.

"You've got some beautiful trails around here," she said. "I've been meaning to ask you about the restaurants in town. I'd like to go someplace special tonight."

Alex wanted to recommend Monet's Garden to her, but until Monet turned things around, Alex owed his first loyalty to his guests. "Mama Ravolini's is a great place if you like Italian. Buck's Grill is fine for burgers and fries, but it's not exactly a fancy eatery."

Claudia said, "What about this Monet's Garden I've been hearing about? He's here again today, isn't he? I saw him drive up when I walked past the inn a few minutes ago. I thought you two were friends."

"We just met the other night," Alex said. "But you must be mistaken. This is the first time he's ever been to Hatteras West."

Claudia looked surprised. "Are you sure? I could have sworn I saw him out here in his car a few days ago."

"When exactly did you see him?" Alex asked.

"I'm certain it was the day of the murder," Claudia said. "I'm not likely to ever forget that. Well, I'd better go to my room and change. I'm going to Hickory today and do some shopping."

As Alex finished his dusting, he wondered if Claudia could be mistaken, or if Monet had visited the inn before. But why would he lie about something like that? It just didn't make sense. Alex knew it would gnaw at him until he knew, but as he started for his office, the telephone at the front desk rang.

"Alex, this is Vince Darcy."

"What can I do for you?"

"I hate to ask," Vince said, "but we're out of towels. Laura got a little carried away."

Alex said, "I'll be right up." He retrieved a new set from the linen closet upstairs and delivered them to the couple. By the time he got back downstairs, Monet was gone. Alex would have to ask him about his visits to Hatteras West later.

"So what did you tell him?" Alex asked Elise when he saw her later.

"Mostly I listened," Elise said. "He's going straight to Irma's. I called her, and she's willing to help."

"She's got a good heart, even if it ends up ruining her. Did Monet say anything about being out here at the inn before today?"

Elise said, "No. In fact, he made a point to mention this was his first visit here. Why?"

"Oh, it's nothing," Alex said, trying to dismiss it.

Elise wasn't buying it, though. "What's going on, Alex?"

"Claudia Post just told me she saw Monet out here the day of the murder. If that's true, why has he been making such a fuss about this being his first visit?"

"That is odd," Elise said. "Could Claudia have been mistaken?"

"It's possible, I guess. She saw him from the walking trail, and Monet's a hard man to miss between that gleaming bald head and his handlebar mustache. I can't think of a soul in Elkton Falls who looks anything like him."

"You've got a point there."

Melva Flump interrupted them, her game of backgammon with Laura Darcy completed. "Excuse the interruption, but I seem to be out of postcards."

Alex knew why, but he promised them to his guests, even if this one was trying to go through an entire print run herself.

Elise said, "Of course. Come with me and I'll get you some."

Alex wondered what adventures Melva would be writing about tonight as Elise led her to their supply closet. He'd have to check the level of their inventory and order more if Melva was going to stay on. Alex put Monet out of his mind, promising himself to talk with the man again and ask him about Claudia's account of his prior visit.

For now, he had an inn to run.

Alex was surprised to find Rose Lane waiting for him at the front desk.

"It's good to see you back."

"I'm looking for a job," she said brusquely.

"Any one in particular?" Alex asked.

"I used to be a maid. Was one for years. This place is too big for two people to run." She took a breath, looked around, then said, "If you want to treat your guests right, anyway."

Alex wished he could dispute her statement, but it was all too true. With just he and Elise running Hatteras West now that both buildings were reopened for guests, it was all they could do to perform their regular tasks, not even taking into account adding those special touches that made folks want to come back.

Alex said, "I wish I could offer you something, but I just don't have the budget for it."

Rose said, "Those muffins you've been buying are pretty pricey. Maybe you could cut back on them and bring me on part-time. I work cheap and hard."

Alex said, "I really am sorry, but it's not that simple. Our guests expect their continental breakfast, it's part of what we offer here. Tell you what, I'll keep you in mind if we ever decide to increase our staff."

She snorted once, then said, "Since I'm here, how about if I check the place out?"

"Didn't you look around when you were here to see the Carolina Rhapsody?" Alex asked. He remembered Cliff asking her to step away from the rope, and her disgruntled reply.

"I was here for the emerald, not for the inn."

Alex said, "Be my guest then, look around all you'd like."

After she tottered off, Elise approached. "What did she want?"

"She was looking for a job," Alex said simply.

She raised one eyebrow. "I didn't realize you were hiring."

"Come on, you know better than that. I can barely afford to pay the two of us. And even if I was looking for more staff, there's no way in the world I wouldn't run it past you first. You're head of personnel, didn't I tell you?"

She said, "Wow, does that come with a raise?"

"All the muffins you can eat," he said, and she laughed.

"That's the best offer I've had in a while. So if you didn't offer her a job, what's she doing now?"

"I told her she could look around while she was here."

Elise started after her, and Alex asked, "Where are you going?"

"I want to see what she's up to."

Alex shook his head after Elise was gone. Following Rose Lane around Hatteras West was the last thing he wanted to do. Life was too short to add any more misery to it that wasn't necessary.

Alex had just finished checking the next night's reservations, as few as there were, when the front door to the inn banged open and Reston Shay walked in, an entire crew of men and women dressed in white coveralls following closely on his heels. They had the most thorough assortment of pails, brooms, vacuums, and cleaning supplies he'd ever seen outside of a supply catalogue.

"Reston, welcome back," Alex said. He nodded toward

the people milling behind the millionaire and asked, "What have we here?"

"My crew. I'll be with you in a minute." He turned to the folks behind him and said, "Let's go, people. It's down the hall to the right, room number 3."

Before Reston could deploy his cleaning troops, Alex saw Rose Lane duck her head and bustle past them as she hurried for the door. Elise, close on her heels, followed without a word to Alex. He would love to know what was going on, but he had Reston to deal with at the moment.

"We cleaned your room earlier," Alex said. "There was no need to bring your staff."

"These people aren't on the payroll, at least not permanently. They're specialists, Alex." Reston got close to him, then asked softly, "Have you been in my room after I left my message, Alex? When I give an order, I expect it to be honored."

"I don't doubt it for a second," Alex said. "We haven't been in your room since you called." With the exception of the foray he and Elise had taken inside to check on Reston, it was true.

"Good, good," Reston said, banging Alex's shoulder, the smile back on his face. "No offense, I'm sure you and Elise do a fine job around here, but I've got the best people working for me. They'll give me just the service I demand."

"And pay handsomely for," Alex said.

"Now don't get your shorts in a knot, son, there's no intentional slam there."

"None taken. Since your crew has your room covered, I hope you'll excuse me. I've got sheets to fold."

Reston either missed or chose to ignore the ice in Alex's voice. "Good man. Keep at it, then."

Before he could get away, Reston asked, "Has that insurance man been back out here?"

"No, I heard he was still in town, though."

"That man's like a tick," Reston said. "He just won't let go."

Before Shay could go on another diatribe, Alex retreated to the laundry room and pulled a load of sheets from the dryer. He was still folding when Elise came in, a look of triumph on her face.

"What's behind that smile?" he asked her.

"I caught our would-be maid snooping around Reston Shay's door. She was trying to get in, and when I called her on it, she shot past me and bolted for the door. I caught up with her in the parking lot. She denied everything, said she was lost and thought it was a restroom, but I don't believe it, not for one second."

Alex said, "Elise, she could have been lost. I've had folks lose sight of the lighthouse when they're sitting on the front porch, and it's right there in front of them."

"She's up to something, Alex."

"Do you have any proof?" he asked.

"Just a feeling in my gut," she said. "If she comes back, let me know, would you?"

"I promise. In the meantime, we don't have to worry about Reston Shay or his room. He's got his cleaning crew in there now scouring the place."

"Was that the crowd out in the lobby? I thought we were being invaded by a Mr. Clean convention."

"Don't laugh, they looked pretty focused."

She said, "I can't believe he doesn't think we're thorough enough in our cleaning. Most likely we're better than his staff."

"I wouldn't bet on it. They looked like cleaning machines. Hey, let's not sweat it. This way we have more time for other things."

"What did you have in mind?" Elise asked.

"I've been meaning to take a crack at the lobby windows, but I never seem to get around to it."

She nodded. "Now you're talking. Tell you what, you do the inside and I'll tackle the outside."

"That's hardly fair, the outside has to be dirtier."

Elise said, "Let's race. Loser buys dinner."

"You're on."

It was a race Alex didn't care who won. Either way, he was going to get to share another meal with Elise. It didn't matter who picked up the check.

She had just beaten him, rather handily at that, when Reston came back into the lobby, his crew behind him.

"Finished already?" Alex asked. "I hope your room is to your satisfaction now."

Reston said, "You know what? It's not. Alex, we need to talk."

"What about?" Alex asked.

"It's about something I lost, something extremely important to me," Reston said. "And I'm not talking about the emerald."

If he'd been trying to get Alex's attention, he'd succeeded masterfully.

11

"What exactly did you lose?" Alex asked.

Instead of answering, Reston gestured to the crew. "We're finished here. You can leave."

The woman in charge said, "Again, we're sorry we couldn't—"

Reston broke in. "Yes, yes, I'm sure."

After the crew was dismissed, Reston said, "Alex, could we talk out on the porch?"

"Sure thing," Alex agreed as he followed Reston Shay outside. Once they were on the porch, Alex again noticed how the paint was bare on parts of the lighthouse. He knew he really should get it repainted, but without another major windfall, one he couldn't predict or count on, the cost was beyond his means. He'd even gone so far as to get an estimate from the folks who painted the Outer Banks Hatteras lighthouse the year before, and found the $72,000 quote way too high for his meager budget. He loved owning Hatteras West, but sometimes the prospect of maintaining the property was overwhelming.

Reston Shay took one of the rockers, and Alex sat in the one beside him.

The rich man had wanted to talk to Alex in private, but he was having a tough time getting started. Alex knew better than to break the silence. Reston would tell him when he was ready.

Finally, Reston said, "I feel like a fool coming to you like this, but I don't know what else to do. Alex, can you keep a secret?"

"I can be trusted, if that's what you're asking, but if you're not sure of that, maybe you'd better not tell me."

Reston waved a hand in the air. "I trust you. I don't have much choice, do I?"

"How can I say, until I know what we're talking about?"

Reston nodded. "You've got a point. Alex, let me ask you a question. Do you believe in luck? Good or bad, talismans that can help or hurt you?"

Alex studied his hands a moment before answering. "I understand how a lot of people embrace them, but no, I've never believed in rabbit's feet or four-leaf clovers. I believe we have a hand in our own destinies."

Reston nodded. "Certainly, I agree with that as well. But there are some objects, some things, that seem to be inherently lucky. Believe it or not, I found such an object."

Alex thought it was a load of hogwash, but it wouldn't be diplomatic to tell Reston Shay that, so he merely shrugged as he looked at the lighthouse.

"I lost my touchstone, and a few hours later that guard was dead and the Carolina Rhapsody was stolen. You can't tell me that's just a coincidence."

Alex said the only thing he could think of. "It's not up to me to say. So what is this talisman you lost?" It suddenly dawned on Alex what this was all about, including the cleaning crew that had just left the inn. He added, "No, don't tell me," as he reached into his pocket, took out the scored piece of metal he'd found in the display room, and dropped it in Reston's hand.

Reston Shay looked incredulously at Alex, then stroked the steel delicately with his fingertips, an expression of rapturous glee on his face. "How did you know it was mine? Where did you find it?"

Alex said, "I was cleaning the room before you decided to stay there and I found it by the grate. What exactly is it?"

Reston held the piece up between his forefinger and thumb and said, "It's a meteorite, Alex. I don't know what it is about this piece, but it gives off energy to whoever holds it. Didn't you feel it?"

Alex shook his head. "Sorry. Maybe you have to be a believer for it to work."

Reston Shay shook his head. "It doesn't matter. What counts is that you found it. The reward I offered that crew belongs to you."

The man pulled out his wallet and removed five crisp new hundreds and handed them toward Alex.

"I can't accept that," Alex said. "I was just doing my job. You lost something at my inn, and I returned it."

"I insist," Reston said. "You can't imagine what you've done for me."

Alex tried not to look at the extended bills. He could certainly use the finder's fee, but his conscience wouldn't let him. If Elise had found the metal herself, he would have had no problem with her taking the money, but there was a difference between them; she was an employee, no matter how valuable, but he was the owner.

When Reston saw that Alex wasn't going to take the money, he put the bills back in his wallet, then said, "If you won't accept my money, I'll find another way to make it up to you."

"It's really not necessary," Alex said. "I'm glad to help."

"I know it's not necessary," Reston said, a spark of anger coming through his voice. "But it's something I need to do." He tossed the metal up in the air, grabbed it with delight, then put it in his pocket. "Things are going to work out, Alex, you mark my words."

As the rich man headed for the parking lot, Alex called out, "Will you be staying here with us tonight?"

"You never know. I never know myself. Thanks again, my friend." He paused, then added, "By the way, I'd appreciate it if we kept this between ourselves. It's hard to explain, if you know what I mean."

"It's already forgotten," Alex said. He wasn't about to advertise the fact that he'd just turned down five hundred dollars because of his stubborn streak of pride. Reston Shay was allowed his foibles just as much as Alex was allowed his.

At least it cleared up one of the mysteries at Hatteras West. He only wished the rest of the puzzles could be solved so easily.

The next morning as Alex was making his cleaning rounds, he had a tough time not staring at the bathroom in Patrick Thornton's room. He'd managed to suppress his curiosity about the tube he and Elise had found hidden in the toilet tank, but the proximity of it was driving him crazy.

He had to know what was in it. With duct tape and plastic from the supply closet, he should be able to cover his tracks and rewrap the packet as he'd found it, but even if he couldn't, it was a chance he was going to have to take.

After deadbolting the door, Alex felt his hands shake as he lifted the lid of the toilet.

It was empty! Thornton must have moved his secret stash somewhere else. But why? Surely the small distance Alex had moved the tube wasn't discernable. Perhaps Thornton moved the tube every so often out of caution. Alex did a rather thorough search of the room, but if the tube was still there, he wasn't able to find it. He did stumble across a sheaf of maps and a few chunks of rock, but nothing helped him determine exactly what he'd been looking for.

At the owner's insistence, Alex and Elise had agreed to lunch at Monet's Garden. He'd discuss the situation with her then. Normally Alex and Elise would never leave the inn together at noon when they had a healthy stream of guests, but on occasion they made an exception; otherwise, they would never have a chance to be together away from the inn. As much as Alex loved Hatteras West, and most especially the lighthouse, there were times when he just had to get away, if only for an hour or two. Maybe Harry's offer of an inn swap would do them both good. It was one more thing to discuss with Elise over lunch.

After his rooms were cleaned, he went in search of Elise. She had finished before him and was changed and waiting for him behind his desk, going through a stack of bills, organizing them in the order they needed to be paid.

Alex said, "Wow, you're getting faster every day."

"My building's not as full as yours. I've barely got enough to do to keep me busy."

"We could always switch," Alex said, adding a smile.

"And you could take over this," she said.

Alex shook his head. "I take it back. Let's leave things exactly the way they are." Alex had struggled with the sheer volume of bills long before Elise came to Hatteras West. He was notorious for paying them as soon as he got them, as long as he had money in the bank to cover the requested amounts. Elise had shuddered at his system, and had quickly set up a schedule to pay them just before they were due, and no sooner. The interest on their account wasn't much, but every little bit helped.

"I need to take a quick shower and I'll be ready to go," Alex said.

Elise stood. "I'll meet you here. I want to call Emma before we go."

"They're not joining us again, are they?" Alex asked, trying to hide his disappointment. As much as he loved Mor and Emma, it seemed that lately he and Elise were spending all of their free time with the newlyweds.

"No, you're going to have to suffer through lunch with just me. Can you handle it?"

Alex grinned. "I'll find a way to manage. Give me five minutes and I'll be ready."

She looked at the watch pinned to her polo shirt. "You're on the clock. Go."

He was ready with thirty seconds to spare. From experience, Alex knew that the quicker they left, the less chance someone or something at Hatteras West could cancel their plans. He walked Elise out to his gray Ford pickup in the parking lot. The truck had seen better days, probably in the mid eighties, and Alex had briefly considered replacing it when he'd gotten his windfall, but ultimately he'd decided against it. The truck, though it might not have been aesthetically pleasing, ran well and did everything he asked of it, while the inn had been in dire need of a serious cash infusion.

Besides, Elise seemed to like the old truck as much as he did, duct tape on the seats and all. He held the door open for her and she slid in onto the bench seat. As Alex walked around the front of the truck, he tapped the hood lightly.

Once he was in the driver's seat, Elise said, "You always do that, did you realize that?"

"Do what?" Alex asked as he pulled out of the parking lot and headed down Point Road.

"You rub the hood as you walk past. Is it for luck?"

"I'm just checking how much paint I have left," he said.

She laughed softly. "You're as sentimental as I am. Admit it."

"I never denied it."

Alex could feel Elise's gaze on him. "Go ahead, ask."

"What are you talking about?"

Alex said, "I can feel a question in the air."

She nudged his arm. "You think you're so smart."

He waited her out, and in a minute she said, "Okay, I'm dying to know. What was in the tube?"

"Tube?" he asked.

"Alex Winston, I know you better than that. There's no way in the world you could let that tube go unopened. I rushed through my rooms, then waited all morning for you to come tell me, and I can't wait any longer. What was in there?"

Alex admitted, "I was ready to open it, but Thornton beat me to it. It was gone."

"Did you search his room? He may have moved it. Strike that, I know you looked, I would have torn the place apart myself. Oh Alex, I hope it wasn't drugs."

"There are a thousand things I hope it wasn't. All I want now is that it's gone for good. Whatever it was, my gut tells me it couldn't have been something I wanted at Hatteras West."

"I think we still need to keep our eye on Patrick. I saw him a little bit ago."

Alex took a second and glanced over at her. "Today?"

"Just before we left. There's something I don't understand. I thought he was supposed to be doing this big survey project?"

"That's what he said," Alex admitted.

"So why is he staying so close to the inn property? If he hasn't been on Winston land the entire time, he's been close enough to see it. Vince Darcy told me he saw Patrick walking through the old orchard with a shovel in one hand and a map in the other."

"Maybe he was looking for a surveyor's point," Alex said. "Parts of that orchard are pretty overgrown."

"I guess so," Elise said as he pulled up in front of

Monet's Garden. The parking lot was practically empty, and Alex wondered if it was because of the food or the steep prices. Either way, something was going to have to change if Monet was going to stay in Elkton Falls.

As they walked in, Alex wondered if they should have dressed up more than they had, but it was too late to do anything about that now.

Monet met them as if they were long lost friends. "Alex, Elise, I'm so glad you have agreed to join me for lunch."

So much for privacy, Alex thought as Monet led them to a table by the expanse of windows. The two men fought to hold Elise's chair for her, finally splitting the duty. He saw Elise fight a smile, but she didn't say a word.

"So how are things going?" Elise asked the restaurateur. "Did you talk to Irma?"

"The woman is a font of information. And she shares it so willingly! A saint walking among us, that is Irma Bean."

Alex would have described Irma a thousand different ways without saint ever coming up in the conversation, but for Monet, she was probably just that. "I'm glad she could help you," Alex said.

"Help? I should make her a silent partner. Already her suggestions are paying great dividends."

Alex looked around the restaurant, barely attended by a few business people and one elderly woman from town who had a fortune of her own and never ate at home.

Monet said, "Don't let this deceive you. Monet's Garden is going to succeed now, I know it." A college-aged girl hovered nearby, clearly uncertain what to do with the restaurant owner seated at one of her tables. Monet waved her over and said, "Today, they dine with my pleasure. There will be no bill for this table."

Alex said, "Honestly, we don't mind paying for our meal."

Monet held a hand up. "No more will be said of this. Enjoy, and tell your friends." He added with a slight smile,

"Though you may choose to withhold information about the cost of your meal today."

As the owner left them, Alex studied the menu and was surprised to find that the offerings had indeed changed. Escargot was no longer on the menu, replaced by loaded potato skins. It wasn't that there wasn't a market for snails in Elkton Falls, but the appeal of the skins had to be a little more reaching. There were substitutions throughout the menu, while the restaurant still retained enough of its past fare to please the gourmets in attendance. The prices, in most cases, had been adjusted as well, bringing them more in line with the going rates in Elkton Falls. Alex could see Irma's touch everywhere, and marveled again over the woman's generosity in sharing.

Elise said, "I think I'll have a bowl of the broccoli and cheese soup."

"That's it?" Alex asked.

"What are you going to have?" she asked him.

Alex pretended to study the menu. "I can't decide, but since it's on the house, I thought I might try one of everything. What do you say, are you up for it?"

"Not if I want to walk out of here under my own power. You're not serious, are you?"

"No, I suppose not. I've just never had an offer like this before. Why don't we share the appetizer platter, then you can have your soup and I'll get something else, maybe sirloin tips. Then if we're still hungry, we can have dessert."

Their food, much improved from their last visit, came out promptly and without fanfare. It was delicious, and by some tacit agreement, Alex and Elise kept their small talk away from inn business and murder. Monet, obviously fighting the urge to hover, joined them as soon as they finished their meals.

"And was everything to your satisfaction?" he asked nervously.

"It was wonderful," Elise said.

"Alex?"

He nodded. "I think you're going to be just fine. For what it's worth, I heartily approve."

Monet clapped his hands. "Excellent. You must try the dessert. It is the richest cheesecake you will ever taste in your life. It is so good, it will make you cry."

Alex said, "We'll have to take a rain check. We're both pretty full."

Monet said sadly, "But I made it myself, in your honor."

Alex was about to protest when Elise said, "Bring us one serving and two forks."

Monet, not giving them the opportunity to change their minds, raced off to the kitchen and was back before Alex could raise another halfhearted protest. Thank goodness they had a light workload at the inn that afternoon. He wasn't sure how much work he'd be able to do, waddling around the place after eating so much.

The cheesecake was everything as promised, drizzled lightly with a chocolate and raspberry glaze. When they were through, Alex found himself wishing for another portion, despite how full he felt.

Monet nodded approvingly as he approached them. "You are satisfied?"

"It was wonderful," Alex said.

Elise added, "Sometime you'll have to give me a lesson in making your cheesecake."

"Irma has told me of your prowess in the kitchen," Monet said. "It would be an honor."

Alex said, "Are you sure about the check?"

Monet said, "Please, do not insult me. This was my gift to the two of you."

"And we thank you kindly for it," Elise said as she stood. "But we really must be getting back to Hatteras West."

"That I understand. Give me one moment, I beg of you." Monet signaled to their waitress, who joined them promptly with a box in her hands.

"What's this?" Alex said as he took the offering.

"In case you get peckish this evening, I took the liberty of packaging the rest of your cheesecake."

"I should offer at least a little resistance," Alex said. "But I'm afraid you might change your mind."

Monet laughed heartily. "You are clearly a man after my own heart. Now come again, with your friends next time. That card is still good for all of you."

"We will," Elise said as they walked out.

Driving back to the inn, the cheesecake safely on Elise's lap, Alex said, "Mor's not going to believe this."

"That you went back to the restaurant?"

Alex said, "No, that I got a free meal and he didn't."

"Oh Alex. Do you have to tell him?"

He tapped the box lightly and smiled. "Absolutely, but not until this is gone. Otherwise I'd have to share."

"You mean we, don't you?"

Alex tapped the steering wheel. "That's exactly what I mean. I can't think of a better dinner, can you?"

"We need something besides this," Elise said.

"You're right, of course. How about two glasses of milk?" Elise laughed softly. "It was wonderful, wasn't it?"

Alex agreed. "I'm not sure I want you to learn how to make it, though."

"Why ever not?"

"I'll have to walk the lighthouse steps four times a day if I eat something that rich as often as I'd like to. I'm going to be worthless this afternoon as it is."

"You'll have to muddle through somehow," she said. "There's laundry to be done, and I need to take a stab at the windows on the second floor. I can't believe how fast they get dirty."

But their plans for the afternoon were suddenly shattered as they came up Point road. There, in front of the inn, was an ambulance, the lights on top flashing in hypnotic warning.

Something had gone terribly wrong at Hatteras West.

12

As Alex raced for the front door, he nearly collided with the EMS team taking their patient out on a gurney. Alice Parsons and John Sumter had been to the inn before, more than Alex would ever admit to any of his guests. Vince Darcy lay strapped to the gurney, a bloody compress taped to his thigh. The man's face was ghostly pale.

"What happened?" Alex asked.

Vince said, "I can't believe it. I was out running and somebody shot me."

Alex asked, "Did you see who did it?"

Vince shuddered once, then said, "No, I was in the woods, and you know how dense it is. Listen, I need somebody to go tell Laura. She's in town shopping."

"We'll find her," Elise said as she rushed up beside Alex. "Are you going to be okay?"

"It hurts like a dog, but they tell me I'm going to be fine," Vince said. "Man, I'm not going to be able to run for a month."

"Another three or four inches and you wouldn't have

been able to make it back to the inn," one of the attendants said. "You were lucky."

"I wasn't lucky enough for them to miss."

As they loaded Vince into the ambulance, Alex asked Alice, "Will he be okay?"

"It's not for me to say, but it looks like the bullet just grazed him."

"My leg's killing me, there's nothing 'just' about that," Vince protested.

Alice shrugged. "It's probably going to leave a scar, but John's right; Mr. Darcy, you're luckier than you realize."

Alex asked, "Did anybody call Armstrong?"

"One of his deputies is on the way."

"Thanks for showing up so fast," Alex said to them as they closed the ambulance door. After the vehicle took off, Alex told Elise, "I'd better go into town and find Laura. Do you want to ride in with me?"

Elise said, "I'd like to, but somebody needs to stay behind and take care of things here."

Alex nodded. "We can swap jobs if you'd like."

Elise said, "No thanks, I'd rather not have to tell a guest her husband was shot at the inn."

"Yeah, you've got a point. I'll be back as soon as I can find her."

"Call me if you hear anything else about Vince," she said.

"I promise. And Elise? Maybe you should stay away from cleaning windows this afternoon."

"You can't think I'm in danger of being shot, Alex. Surely this was just an unfortunate accident."

"You're probably right, but I'd feel better if you stayed inside," Alex said.

"I will. There's plenty for me to do around here."

As Alex drove back to town in search of Laura, he tried to think who might have shot his guest. Could it have been an accident, as Elise clearly thought, some fool plinking cans in the woods without realizing how far his bullets traveled, or was it something more sinister than that? Had Vince, in his incessant jogging around the lands that encircled the inn, stumbled across something he shouldn't have seen? No, Alex realized it was most likely an accident. After all, there wasn't anything going on around Hatteras West that he didn't know about. At least he didn't think so.

Alex scanned the parked cars in Elkton Falls, searching for Laura's car as he drove through town. He found it parked in front of Shantara's General Store, the third place he looked.

Laura was looking at a display of hand-fired pottery.

"I need a second," he said to her as he touched her arm.

"Hi, Alex. Tell me, which do you like better, the green glaze or the blue?"

"Vince's been shot," he said.

The plate fell to the floor, shattering on the hardwood. That got everyone's attention, including Shantara's. Alex held a hand up toward her as he said to Laura, "The paramedics said it was just a graze. He got lucky. Vince lost some blood, but it looks like he's going to be all right."

"I told him jogging was going to kill him someday. Maybe now he'll listen to me. Is he at the hospital yet?"

"They left ahead of me, so they've got to be there by now. Why don't you let me drive you over there, and we can pick up your car later."

"No, I know where the place is, I passed it on the way in. I'll drive myself."

Alex said, "I'm really sorry about this."

"Unless you're the one who shot him, you don't have anything to apologize for." She rushed out, leaving Alex and Shantara standing nearby.

He said, "Sorry about that. Why don't you add that to

my bill? I should have found a better way to break the news to her."

Shantara grabbed a broom and started sweeping up the shards. "It wouldn't have been a bad idea to at least grab the plate first. Is her husband really going to be all right?"

"It looks like it," Alex said.

Shantara shook her head. "See? That's why I don't exercise. There's too much risk involved."

"Let me get this straight," Alex said to his old friend. "You don't jog so you won't get shot?"

"Hey, if your guest had come shopping with his wife in my store instead of going out for a run, none of this would have happened."

Alex said, "And you wouldn't be out one plate."

"No, my friend, *you* wouldn't be out one plate. You offered to pay for it, remember?"

Alex nodded. "I did at that."

Shantara slapped his arm. "Don't look so glum, I'll just charge you wholesale."

"You're all heart," Alex said.

Shantara asked, "So how was lunch at Monet's Garden? Better than the dinner I had there, I hope."

"Now how did you know I ate there for lunch?" Alex asked. "Elise and I left the restaurant not half an hour ago."

Shantara said, "I was at the bank making a deposit and I happened to see you and Elise leaving from across the street. Hey, it's a small town, Alex."

"And getting smaller by the minute," he said. "I'd better get back to the inn."

"So you can post some 'No Hunting Guests' signs?" she asked.

"Now that you mention it, that's not a bad idea."

Shantara shrugged. "I was just kidding. Besides, hunting season hasn't even started yet."

"That's what I'm afraid of," Alex said as he left the store. It was time to go see the sheriff. Maybe while he was

there he could see if there were any breaks in the case of
the missing emerald or the dead security guard.

Alex found Armstrong sitting behind his desk, talking on the telephone with his feet propped up on the file
cabinet beside the desk. The sheriff didn't hear Alex come
in, that much was obvious from the way he spoke to the receiver.

"Now Betty Lou, we don't have to go to Buck's, not if
you don't want to. Monet's Garden? I heard it wasn't very
good. No, I don't mind how expensive it is." The sheriff
grimaced at that outright lie. "If that's the only place you'll
go out with me, I'm willing to give it a try." The sheriff
was making a hard play for Betty Lou Jackson. He was
more serious than Alex realized, since Armstrong was no-
toriously tight with his money.

The sheriff swiveled around in his chair as he pulled his
feet off the cabinet and saw Alex standing there. With a
cough and a deepening of his voice, Armstrong said,
"Seven it is. See you then."

After the sheriff hung up the telephone, he looked at
Alex and said, "Before you say a word, I've got one of my
men out at the inn even as we speak. No doubt somebody
was taking some target practice, Alex. You should tell your
guests if they're going to be trotting around in the woods,
they need to wear some blaze orange so folks can see
them."

Alex knew if he rose to the bait, Armstrong would get
huffy and clam up about everything. "As long as you're
looking into it, it's okay with me. Is there anything new on
Cliff's murder and the emerald theft?" Alex asked.

"We're following some leads right now, that's all I'll
say," Armstrong said huffily. So he didn't have a clue.

"Have they all been dead ends?" Alex asked sympa-
thetically.

Armstrong shrugged. "We won't know till we finish our investigation. Is that why you're here, to check up on me?"

Alex said, "One of my guests was shot half an hour ago at the inn. That alone gives me the right to be here."

"Calm down, Alex. Just before you came in, I got a call from the hospital, and they said he was shot in the thigh. It was just a flesh wound, it barely nicked him."

"What if it wasn't an accident?" Alex blurted out, despite his promise not to aggravate the sheriff any more than he had to.

"You have any reason to believe that?" Armstrong asked.

Alex admitted, "No, no reason I can put my finger on."

"Then until you do, I suggest you stop talking like it was intentional. What are you trying to do, Alex, shut yourself down? You honestly think many folks are going to want to stay with you at the lighthouse if there's a fool taking shots at your guests? I think you'd better leave that dog alone."

Alex said, "I can't do that, not if there's a chance it wasn't an accident."

Armstrong shrugged. "It's your funeral. Tell you what, I'll drive out to the inn and look around some if it will make you feel any better. Where exactly was he shot?"

"He said he was near the woods by the orchard," Alex said. "If you want, I can walk out there with you." Alex wanted a first-hand look at where Vince had been jogging when he'd been shot.

"Naw, I think I can handle this by myself. I'll try to make it out there before dark. I appreciate the help, much as I don't need it, but you've got an inn to run, don't you?"

"Just let me know if you find anything," Alex said.

Armstrong nodded. "I'll do it."

Alex would have to be satisfied with that. As he drove back to Hatteras West, he wondered what, if anything, the sheriff would find, and more importantly, if he really would share the information with Alex. The two men had worked together in the past on some of Armstrong's cases, but that didn't necessarily mean that it would continue.

Elise had just finished mopping the lobby when Alex walked in.

"There must have been more blood than I remembered," he said.

Elise answered, "I couldn't just mop part of the floor, you know me better than that. So did you find Laura?"

"She was at Shantara's, and the last I saw of her, she was on her way to the hospital."

Elise said, "I've been thinking. You're probably right about it not being an accident. You really should talk to the sheriff about this."

Alex nodded. "I just came from there. He seems to think somebody was outside fooling around with their gun, but he's agreed to look around later."

"I'm surprised you're satisfied with that," Elise said.

"Hey, we've got an inn to run, remember? Armstrong can handle this by himself."

Elise patted his arm. "He wouldn't let you go with him, would he?"

Alex chuckled softly. "You're getting to know me too well, you realize that, don't you?"

Elise said, "I don't know about that. I just know how you think."

"I'm not sure which one of us should be more frightened by that prospect," Alex said as Claudia Post came into the lobby.

"If it's not too much trouble, I'm completely out of towels again," she said, then turned and headed back to her room. The woman went through laundry like boiling water through snow since the wine explosion. At least she'd recovered most of her hearing.

Elise said, "I'll be right there." As she left, trying to catch up with their guest, Elise glanced back at Alex and smiled. Whenever she did that, even if circumstances didn't necessarily warrant it, Alex felt that all was right with the world.

At least for the moment the smile lasted on her lips.

A few hours later, Vince and Laura came back to Hatteras West. His sweat pants had been replaced by a set of doctor's scrubs, and there were a few crimson stains on his shirt.

Laura said, "I hope you don't mind, Alex, but we're checking out a few days early."

"It's not a problem at all," Alex said as she headed upstairs to pack their bags while Vince stayed behind in the lobby.

After Laura was gone, Alex said, "I completely understand you wanting to leave. Listen, I'm really sorry about all this."

Vince sat in one of the lobby chairs and said, "Hey, things happen. I'd feel better being home, that's all."

"And the doctors don't have a problem with you leaving?" Alex asked.

Vince said, "They told me I should be fine. It was just a graze after all. Besides, we're not driving all the way back home tonight." He added apologetically, "In all honesty, I just don't want to hang around here and give somebody another shot at me."

Alex nodded. He could hardly blame his guest for not wanting to stay. People had left the inn with a lot less cause than Vince and Laura had. "Thanks for staying with us," Alex said.

Laura came downstairs soon enough with both their suitcases.

Alex said, "At least let me get those for you."

"I can manage," Laura said gruffly.

Alex insisted, saying, "You should help your husband. I'll get the bags."

Laura's stern expression softened. "Of course you're right. Thank you."

Alex nodded and walked them out to their car. Vince was still noticeably limping, and he saw that Laura had pillows arranged in the back seat. As Vince eased onto them, he said, "With her pampering me like this, I'm going to milk this for all it's worth."

Laura said, "You've got a free pass for the time being, so you may as well take advantage of it."

After they were gone, Elise was waiting for Alex in the lobby. "Did someone check out?" she asked.

"The Darcys decided to cut their stay short," Alex admitted.

"What a relief," Elise said.

"And what did you have against the Darcys that you're so happy they've left us?"

Elise swatted him with the dusting rag in her hand. "If he's well enough to travel, the injury must not have been all that serious. It could have been a great deal worse, you know that, don't you?"

"I don't even want to think about it," Alex said. "Now what do we have left to do?"

"Thanks to Claudia Post, we have another load of towels to run through the laundry. Besides that, we've just about got everything knocked out for the day."

Alex said, "Tell you what, let's start the load of towels, then we can get the lighthouse windows cleaned. You've been after me for a month to do it."

"You're not worried about somebody taking a shot at us up there?" Elise asked.

"No, I can't imagine anyone trying it. One thing's for sure; if they do, we'll know it's no accident, not at that angle."

"It's a deal," Elise said.

They gathered their cleaning supplies and were heading

out the door when Skip Foreman, the ex-cop on Reston Shay's security team, walked in.

"Is this a bad time?" he asked.

"No, we were just going to start on some windows. What can we do for you?"

The big man frowned, then said, "I understand there was a shooting out here today. How's your guest doing?"

"He's going to be fine, it was just a graze," Alex said. "As a matter of fact, he's on his way back home right now."

Skip said, "I'm sorry to hear that."

"What, that he's gone? I can't blame him for not hanging around here after being shot."

"That's not what I meant," the retired deputy said. "I was hoping to get a chance to talk to him, but I was too late to make it to the hospital in time."

Elise asked, "You don't think it was an accident, do you?"

"Now, Ma'am, I didn't say that."

Alex said, "But you're here nonetheless. I take it you're not buying the sheriff's explanation."

Skip didn't answer the question. "I just wanted to clear a few things up for my own curiosity. Sorry I bothered you folks."

Alex said, "I'm just wondering, what would you have asked him?"

"Like I said, it was nothing official," Skip said, but Alex wasn't going to let it go that easily.

Alex said, "I spoke with him. I know third-hand information wouldn't be of any use in court, but I still might be able to help."

Skip shrugged. "Do you know where exactly he was shot?"

Elise said, "The leg. Oh, of course that's not what you meant. It was somewhere out in the woods."

"Ma'am, there are a ton of woods around this place. Can you be more specific?"

Alex said, "Near the orchard. It had to be, from what he told me. That was the route he took every morning. He ran around the lighthouse, lapped Bear Rocks, then went through the orchard before he wound up back at the inn. The blood splatters we saw came from the direction of the orchard too; otherwise he'd have used the back porch door. There's no way he'd walk around the inn to use the front door, not shot and bleeding, and that's exactly what he would have had to do if he'd been coming from Bear Rocks."

Skip nodded. "Makes sense. You ever been in law enforcement?"

Alex felt his face redden. "Hardly. It just seems logical that way."

"So it does. Let me ask you both something. Is there anything strange that's been going on around the inn lately? I mean besides the murder and theft."

Elise said, "We can't help you there. There's always something odd going on around Hatteras West. Take your pick."

Alex started to say something about the tube they'd found in Patrick Thornton's toilet tank, but without anything more solid than their suspicions, he didn't feel right disclosing that information. From the look Elise was giving him, evidently she felt the same way.

If Skip noticed the exchange, he didn't mention it. "I think I'll snoop around a little out there, if you don't mind."

"The orchard's not Winston land anymore, but I don't think the owner would mind. He's been in Florida for as long as I can remember, and he lets me pick all the fruit I want from the trees. Help yourself."

"I'll do just that."

Before Skip could leave, Elise said, "There is one thing."

"What's that?" the former deputy asked.

"If you find anything, let us know, okay?"

Skip grinned. "It's probably a blind alley, but I'll tell you if I stumble across something."

After he was gone, Alex and Elise tackled the first row of windows at the top of the lighthouse. He was awfully glad they could clean them from the narrow walkway that was just above the observation platform. The glass was sparkling when Alex and Elise finished the bottom row and were ready to start on the next level when they both heard someone hailing them from below. Skip was on the front porch, and Alex and Elise hurried down the stairs to meet him.

"Did you find anything?" Alex asked, nearly out of breath.

"There weren't any old tin cans or shot-up trees out there, not that I could see."

"Maybe you weren't looking in the right place," Elise said.

"I found blood on some of the leaves and the spot where your jogger hit the ground. I did a pretty thorough search around the area, but there was nothing else out of the ordinary that I could spot."

Elise said, "So Sheriff Armstrong was right, it most likely was an accident."

"Just the opposite," Skip said. "I'd say that shot was dead-on intentional."

13

"How do you figure that?" Alex asked.

"If I'd seen any indication that someone had been shooting up cans or even taking potshots at trees, I'd buy the accidental shooting theory. But there wasn't a sign of it anywhere in the woods that I could see, and I've got a pretty good eye for that kind of thing. Even a tin can hit by a bullet will throw off some metal, but I didn't see any sign of it. Think about it. If it was harmless target practice, why would they bother cleaning up after themselves? Anybody foolish enough to shoot at targets in the woods is bound to be too selfish to clean up after themselves. No, that shot was meant for your guest."

"So what do we do about it?" Alex asked.

Skip said, "There's nothing much you can do but keep your eyes and ears open. Tell you what, I'll nose around town a little and see if I can find out anything else."

"What's Armstrong going to say about that?" Alex asked.

"What can he say? I'm not investigating anything, at least not officially. And if he gives me any grief, I'll just tell him I'm getting the lay of the land. He's already asked me twice if I'm running against him. It's pretty obvious he doesn't believe the answer I keep giving him." Skip stroked his chin. "You know what? Maybe I *will* run against him. I kind of miss being involved in law enforcement. This case has my juices flowing again."

Alex wasn't sure how he felt about the declaration after Skip was gone. He owed Armstrong his loyalty, at least a part of him felt that way, but Skip Foreman had worked high up in a large metropolitan police force, and he had to bring more to the table than Armstrong ever could. In the current sheriff's favor was the fact that he knew the people of Elkton Falls. He'd grown up there and was a solid part of the community. If Skip did decide to run for office the next time around, Alex was going to have a tough time making his pick.

He asked Elise, "So, are you ready to finish those windows?"

She nodded. "I won't be able to sleep tonight, knowing that some of them are still dirty."

"But we're saving the higher glass for another day, right?"

Elise said, "Let's see how long it takes us to finish what we've started."

Alex shook his head. He'd worked with Elise long enough to know that they'd both still be on that catwalk around the lens before the sun set that night. The upper balcony had been constructed to allow the lighthouse keepers to clean the salt spray from the glass surrounding the lens on the original beacon at the Outer Banks, but it worked just as well for cleaning the red clay dust that tended to accumulate over time.

When they finished their exterior cleaning job, Alex was tempted to fire up the lens to see how brilliantly the light would shine, but he'd promised Tracy to keep his hands off the switch until she could talk to the town council about providing him with more opportunities to light it without worrying about getting fined yet again.

That night, tired and sore from the extra exertion of cleaning all that glass, Alex thought he'd fall asleep immediately. Instead, he tossed and turned half the night. Something he'd heard in the past few days was bothering him, but he couldn't put his finger on it.

It made for a restless night, and a weary feeling in his heart the next morning.

Elise was a little less than her usual bright and chipper self at breakfast as well. There was a slight cloud to her smile that he immediately recognized as trouble at Hatteras West.

"What's wrong?" he asked her.

"Fiona's muffins aren't here yet, and some of our guests have been asking for them. They won't even touch Sally Anne's anymore."

Alex said, "Why don't we put out more fruit until they get here?"

"That's not the point, Alex. Fiona should have had them here last night. At the very least, I expected the basket here when I came out this morning, but there's nothing."

Fiona's white van drove up, decorated with dancing muffin magnets attached to its sides.

"Here she is," Alex said as he headed for the door.

Elise cut him off before he could open it. "This is my area of responsibility. I'll take care of it."

Alex watched as Elise approached Fiona, stopping her outside before she could get to the front porch. He was glad he wasn't on the other end of the scolding Fiona was getting, but it didn't appear to have the slightest affect on the Muffin Lady. She listened until Elise was finished, thrust the basket into her arms, then drove off.

"How did that go?" Alex asked as she walked back in.

"I swear, I don't think she heard a word I said. There's something odd about that woman."

"I'm willing to allow her a few eccentricities, as long as I get my muffins." Alex reached in for a pumpkin one, teasing Elise to try and break her dark mood, but she failed to make even a token swat at Alex's hand.

"Hey, if it will cheer you up, we can tackle the lens itself this afternoon, or at least get a good start on it. That's a lot of glass we're talking about there."

She nodded, but her smile was still forced. He fought back the urge to offer her advice on how to handle Fiona. As Elise had pointed out, the continental breakfast they served was her area of responsibility, and there was no way Alex was going to butt in.

He grabbed a glass of orange juice to go with his muffin and walked over to the check-in desk. They had three sets of new guests coming in today, and he wanted to be ready for them.

Later that morning, Alex heard a drill in the hallway outside the room he was cleaning and wondered what was going on. Since he did all the repairs he could handle himself, or called Mor Pendleton if it was over his head, he couldn't imagine what was happening.

Amy Lang, the sculptor and now their sign painter, was pulling the plaque off room seven and replacing it with a much more ornate one. In a flowery script, it said, "The Carolina Jasmine Room."

She grinned when she saw Alex. "So what do you think?"

"Nicely done," Alex said. He admired her work, from the crisply routed edges of the sign to the intricate paint job, but it was going to take some getting used to.

She laughed. "I know you, Alex Winston, you're not a great fan of change, but Elise is right. I think it's a splendid idea."

"You've outdone yourself," Alex admitted. "I hope we didn't keep you from your work."

As she drove in the last screw, Amy said, "I just finished a commission for a house in Hickory, so these signs were a nice break. I just wish the steel I usually work with was as pliable as this wood."

Elise joined them, looked at the sign a second, then hugged Amy. "They're perfect." She glanced at Alex and asked, "Aren't they?"

"Very nice," Alex said.

Amy said, "Don't mind him, they'll grow on him. Now if you two will excuse me, I've got a lot of work to do."

Alex asked, "You've finished them all?"

"As I said, they were fun. Oh, I meant to tell you, I got a letter from Julie Hart. She sends her love."

"How's she doing?" Alex asked. Julie had come to Hatteras West during a difficult time in her life, and Alex hoped all was well with the young woman.

"Never better. She's threatening to come visit again as soon as she gets some vacation time from her new job."

"Let me know and she can stay here with us."

Amy said, "Are you kidding? I'd never get her away from the lighthouse. She was really taken with it."

"It has that affect on some people," Alex admitted.

"Well, enough goofing off. I've got work to do."

As Elise went back to the lobby, Alex told Amy, "They are perfect, you know that, don't you?"

"They'll do," Amy acknowledged as she got back to work. As Alex finished the room he'd been cleaning, number six since he'd been a boy, but soon to be called by another name, he wondered how the line of Winston innkeepers before him would have felt about the change. It was something he always tried to consider before doing anything too different. After all, the inn was more than just a business to him. It was his home, his inheritance, his history.

As he left the room, now christened The Mountain Laurel Suite, Alex admired the signage again. Tracing his fingers over the carefully crafted letters, he had to believe that at least his mother would have approved. She was always in favor of anything that made the inn feel more like a home away from home for their guests. That's why she had spent so many hours crafting the lighthouse quilts for each room. He'd have to speak with Mor soon about building frames for the remaining quilts. That way his mother's hand would still be on Hatteras West, a connection with his past he never wanted to lose.

Alex was surprised to see Patrick Thornton back at the inn early that afternoon. The man's hours normally kept him out during most of daylight.

There was a look of consternation on Thornton's face as he stomped into the lobby.

"Good afternoon," Alex said as pleasantly as he could manage, given his suspicions.

Normally a talkative man, the surveyor just grunted as he passed Alex on the way to his room. There was no doubt about it, something was troubling the man, and Alex wondered if it could have something to do with that missing tube. But how could he find out without tipping his hand? Alex was still considering it when Sheriff Armstrong drove up Point Road and parked in front of the inn.

Alex walked out to greet him. "What brings you out to the inn?"

Armstrong said, "I promised you a progress report, if you still want it. Truth be told, I could use some advice."

Alex fought to hide his smile. "Come on in."

Armstrong shook his head. "Why don't we talk outside? I don't want anybody eavesdropping on us."

Alex led the sheriff over to the lighthouse steps. With their backs to the doors, they could survey the land around them as they spoke.

"So what have you discovered?" Alex asked.

"Precious little, and what there is doesn't make sense.

First let me ask you something. Has that retired deputy been snooping around here?"

"You mean Skip? He's been out here a few times."

Armstrong asked, "What did he want?"

Alex admitted, "He was asking about Vince's shooting."

The sheriff snorted. "I knew it, he's after my job. It was an accident, but he's going to get folks riled up telling them it was deliberate."

"He just wants to know what happened," Alex said gently.

"Let him get in line, I'm still sheriff in Canawba County, and until the folks vote me out, I'm going to run things around here my way."

Alex said, "You said you'd found out a few things about the murder and the theft."

The sheriff nodded. "Okay, let's start with Cliff. Apart from an ex-wife nobody in the county knows, the man led a pretty ordinary life, up until six months ago."

"What changed?" Alex asked.

"All of a sudden he started staying out late and coming home a mess. Melissa Henderson kept better tabs on him than the FBI. Help me from ever having neighbors like her! I went to interview her and ended up staying three hours. I'm amazed she didn't have pictures! The woman keeps a log on all her neighbors, if you can imagine. She said it was better than watching television."

"When you say a mess, what do you mean?"

"She said he was covered in dirt, like he'd been wallowing in the mud. There's a streetlight outside his place, so she's positive about what she saw. And then there were his visitors."

"Did she spot anybody she knew?" Alex asked.

"No, they always came on foot after dark and they seemed to know how to skirt the streetlight, but she said they looked like they were up to no good. I'm not sure if it means anything, Melissa has a pretty active imagination."

"What did you find when you searched his house?"

The sheriff said, "Nothing that struck me as all that odd, but I was wondering if you might want to have a look yourself before his cousin comes for his stuff. He was Cliff's only heir."

There was nothing Alex would like more than to nose around Cliff's apartment. "I can do it tomorrow afternoon right after my rooms are clean."

"By then it will be too late. His cousin's coming first thing in the morning. I was kind of hoping you could come with me now."

Alex said, "Let me talk to Elise. I'll be with you in a few minutes."

He found his head, and only, housekeeper at his desk going through a stack of bills that had just arrived. "Hi, Alex." There must have been something on his face that gave him away. "What's up?"

"I need a few hours. Can you handle the inn?"

"You know I can. Has this got something to do with your talk with the sheriff?"

Alex said, "He's giving me the chance to look over Cliff's house, but it has to be now."

"Any chance I could go with you?" she asked.

"Somebody needs to stay here and watch over the inn," Alex said reluctantly. "We have three sets of guests coming in any time. Do you mind?"

"Hey, you're the boss," Elise said evenly.

"You know what? Come with me. I'll clear it with Armstrong. We can put up a self-serve sign."

"No, I don't mind staying behind."

Alex said, "Really, it's okay."

She smiled softly. "Just knowing that you want me there is enough. You're right, we need to take care of our guests, especially with as many new arrivals as we have coming in. Don't worry, I've got things under control here. But I do expect a full report when you get back."

"Thanks," he said, trying not to shake his head as he walked out. As well as he thought he knew her, sometimes Elise's reaction to things still surprised him. She really had gotten the snooping bug from him.

Armstrong was waiting in the patrol car when Alex came out. He said, "I thought you got lost in your own inn."

"Something came up," Alex said.

"You're good to go, right?"

Alex nodded. "I'm ready."

Once they were there, Armstrong opened Cliff's door for Alex, taking time to wave at Melissa Henderson across the street. "How much you want to bet our little visit is going in the log," the sheriff said.

"She gives a whole new meaning to neighborhood watch, doesn't she?"

"I think she wants me to make her an honorary deputy," Armstrong said as he shut the door behind them. Alex walked through the small place, not knowing just what he was searching for, hoping he'd know it when he saw it. The house was immaculate. There were barely any signs that someone had ever lived there, with the exception of a few pictures on the bedroom dresser. Alex saw a figure carefully cut out of a couple of the group shots, and he pointed it out to Armstrong.

"Yeah, I noticed that. My guess is it was his ex-wife. From what I've heard, their break-up was a bad one."

"Have you talked to her personally?" Alex asked as he put the frame back.

"No, I'm having trouble tracking her down. Alex, they busted up four years ago. You honestly think she waited that long to go after him, and that she happened to have a fake emerald on her to boot? No, I've got to believe Cliff was killed because he was guarding the emerald, not because of anything that happened in his life."

"So why are we here, if you feel that way?"

Armstrong rubbed his chin. "I figured it couldn't hurt, just in case, you know? You've spotted stuff before."

Alex nodded, amazed that the sheriff was openly acknowledging the help he'd given him in the past. Of course, when there were no witnesses around, the sheriff could be quite lavish in his praise, but if a voter was within shouting distance, the compliments trickled down to nothing.

Alex looked in the closet, and took special care to examine the boots there. They were buffed to a high sheen without a trace of dirt or grass anywhere on them. Cliff's dirty-clothes hamper in the bathroom was empty, and Alex figured the man must have just done his laundry before coming to work at the inn the day he died. On the shelves in the living room there were books that covered the gamut from geology to topography, field books on southern forests, meteorology, and star charts. There wasn't a work of fiction in sight. It appeared that Cliff was hooked on natural science, something Alex never would have guessed from his brief acquaintance with the man.

Alex opened the cabinets in the kitchen and found a bachelor's stock of cereal and potato chips, but not much else. There were a few packets of frozen food in the freezer and a spoiled quart of milk in the refrigerator. It appeared that Cliff ate out a lot. Alex would have to talk to Buck and Sally Anne at Buck's Grill to see how well they knew the guard. After all, Cliff had to eat somewhere, and Buck's was about it for breakfast around town.

Armstrong asked Alex, "Do you see anything out of the ordinary?"

Alex shook his head. "Sorry, there's nothing I could see that looked odd."

Armstrong nodded. "I thought as much, but it was

worth a shot. Thanks for coming by. Let me run you back to the inn."

Alex said, "Tell you what, why don't you drop me off at Buck's Grill? I'll grab a ride back from there."

Armstrong said, "It's too late for lunch and not time for supper yet."

"I feel like a piece of peach cobbler," Alex said. Though it was true that Sally Anne made the best cobbler around, it wasn't the only reason he wanted to go to Buck's. There was something about Cliff's place that bothered him. Maybe if he talked to the crew at the diner, he might uncover enough to discover what it was.

14

Alex was glad he'd lucked into visiting at a time when the diner was nearly empty. He was approaching the bar where he usually ate when he was by himself when Sally Anne met him at his stool.

"I'm surprised to see you here during the day," Sally Anne said.

"I had to come by for some of your peach cobbler. Please tell me you made a fresh batch today."

"Peaches aren't in season," Sally Anne said.

Buck poked his head out the order window and said, "Sally Anne, I need to see you back here."

Sally Anne wanted to ignore the summons, Alex could see it in her posture and her eyes, but she knew better than to cross her dad.

Though they kept their voices low, Alex caught a word now and then, just enough for him to realize that Buck was not pleased with his only child, and not afraid of expressing it at all.

Sally Anne came out through the swinging door thirty

seconds later with a healthy slice of peach cobbler in a bowl. "Did you want ice cream with that?"

Alex nodded. "That would be great."

Sally Anne frowned slightly, then returned a minute later with a scoop of vanilla. After dumping it on Alex's cobbler, she turned to go when Alex said, "Do you have a second? I need your help."

Alex saw her glance back to the kitchen, then heard her say, "I'll do what I can."

Alex had been about to ask her about Cliff, but there was something that had to be taken care of first. "Young lady, I've known you since you were knee high to a grasshopper. How long are you going to keep this up?"

Alex saw Buck's head appear in the window again, but the ex-boxer kept quiet.

"It's not fair that a stranger even has a chance to take away my business, Alex," Sally Anne said abruptly. "I had your order first, and you let her swoop in there and steal it from me."

"Sally Anne, if it was peach cobbler I needed, there's none better in seven counties than what you make, but I have to do what's best for my business. Am I sorry that I hurt your feelings? You betcha. Would I do it again? Given the same circumstances, I'm afraid I'd have to. I'm not saying there's anything wrong with your muffins, but it doesn't look like they're going to be able to beat Fiona's. It's that simple. There's nothing personal about it."

Sally Anne threw her dishtowel down. "That's what gets me, Alex, there's nothing personal about it. I thought you were our friend."

Buck started to speak again, but Alex shook his head, and the big man accepted it. Alex was going to have to work this one out on his own if he wanted to keep Sally Anne's friendship. Alex took one of her hands in his and said, "You know we're friends, and we always will be. I was kind of hoping it was enough, all this other business aside."

He thought Sally Anne might pull her hand away, but the two of them had been friends too long, and her stern look gradually dissipated. "As long as you're sure it's not about me," she said.

"Hey, I'm here, aren't I?"

Sally Anne nodded. "Okay, I'll get over it. Now what did you want help with?"

Alex said, "That's going to have to wait one second." He stuck his spoon into the cobbler, snagging a bit of peach along with the golden flaky crust and the melting ice cream. "Ahh," he said as he wiped his mouth. "You are a cobbler genius."

Sally Anne dimpled slightly at the praise. "Okay, enough, we're good again." Buck disappeared back behind the window, but Sally Anne still whispered, "What's going on?"

"Did Cliff Cliff, the security guard, eat much with you'all here?"

Sally Anne said, "If you count every breakfast, some lunches and most dinners. I don't think the man could boil water on his own."

"What did you know about him?" Alex asked.

"Cliff was a creature of habit. He had the same things for every meal he ate here. Oatmeal and toast for breakfast, grilled cheese and tomato soup for lunch, and country-style steak with gravy, mashed potatoes, cooked apples, and a glass of iced tea for dinner. I don't know how he faced it every day."

Alex said, "What about the company he kept? Did he ever eat with anybody in particular?"

Sally Anne shook her head. "He always ate at the bar. If there wasn't a stool open he'd take a table, but the second someone left, he claimed their spot. I'm sorry I'm not much help."

Alex said, "Do me a favor, if you think of anything else, let me know."

"Do you want me to ask around about him?" Sally Anne said.

"No, nothing like that," Alex said quickly. The last thing he needed was for word to get back to Armstrong that he was continuing his own investigation.

She nodded. "Okay, but I can do more than that. All you have to do is ask."

Alex thanked her, and as he ate his cobbler, Sally Anne lingered close by to keep him company. He left a tip as big as his bill, but she wouldn't stand for it. "What's this?" she said, waving the bills at him.

"Hey, I'd have paid twice that for your cobbler."

Sally Anne walked around the counter and tucked half the tip back in Alex's shirt pocket. "Alex Winston, there's no way in the world I'm going to accept that."

That was how Alex knew things were back to normal between the two of them. Buck winked through the window as Alex started to go, and he chuckled softly. It felt right being back on good terms with the pair. He'd meant what he'd said, too. There was no business worth his friendship. Speaking of friends, Alex wasn't all that far from Mor or Les's repair shop. Maybe he could con his best friend into giving him a ride back out to the inn. If not, Alex was sure he could come up with someone in Elkton Falls willing to give him a ride. That was one of the things he liked best about living in the small town. Folks were always willing to lend a hand.

At the fix-it shop, Alex found the senior partner Les sitting at the workbench, the top of it covered with parts from an odd-looking contraption. The handyman was ignoring it though, his feet propped up among the parts and his head buried in a copy of *Modern Candlemaking*.

"I didn't know you made candles," Alex said, knowing

full well that Les Williamson had an addiction to magazines of all sizes and shapes. The school kids of Elkton Falls loved him, knowing that Les was good for at least two subscriptions from every one of them who asked. Alex had actually seen a line of them forming outside the shop the day the fundraiser was announced.

"You have any idea about what goes into making these things?" Les asked, showing Alex an illustrated set of photographs.

"Can't say that I do."

"Well sir, it's tougher than it looks."

"I don't doubt it. Is Mor around?"

Les said, "He'd better not be. I'm still behind from his little honeymoon jaunt, so I've got him burning up the roads. Now that he's a married man, he's not as interested in working as much overtime."

Alex said, "He's got a lot to adjust to. Any idea when he'll be back?"

Les said, "If he doesn't run out of parts, I don't expect him till after five. Was he expecting you, Alex?"

"No, I was just dropping in. I need a ride back out to the inn and I thought he could help me."

Les put his feet on the floor and dropped the magazine to the workbench. "Tell you what, I'll take you myself."

Alex said, "I don't want to keep you from your work, or your reading."

Les grinned. "I could use the excuse. That dadblasted cream separator is giving me fits. I used to be able to fix them blindfolded and half asleep. I must be losing my touch, even if Carole Gentry brought it to me in a box."

"If you're sure you don't mind, that would be great."

"Let me grab my keys," Les said, and Alex waited outside for him to lock up.

Les asked, "What brought you into town without that truck of yours? Don't tell me, it finally died on you, didn't it?"

"No sir, it's running fine. I came in with the sheriff."

Les nodded. "He's working hard to solve that murder you had out your way."

"And the jewel theft, too," Alex added.

Les shook his head. "The murder's the splashy crime for him. I doubt the emerald will ever be found."

Alex noticed the hint of a smile on Les's face. "You don't seem too upset by the prospect."

As they headed toward Hatteras West, Les said, "Reston Shay has been parading that emerald around lately like it was a county fair. Serves him right if he lost it."

"You're not his biggest fan, are you?"

Les tapped the steering wheel. "You could say that. He's a double-dealer and a cheat. Take my advice, Alex, don't ever play cards with him. He'll slip your wallet out of your pocket without you feeling a thing. Nobody at that card table saw him cheat, but he had to have. I just couldn't prove it."

As they passed To Dye For, owned by Irene Wilkins, the town forensics expert and its most popular beautician, Rose Lane walked out, a scarf tied tightly around her hair.

"Well, speak of the devil's handmaids and one of them appears."

Alex asked, "What are you talking about?"

"You know Rose Lane, don't you? She's got a history with Reston herself."

"I hadn't heard. Did they ever go out?"

"Reston and Rose? Not that I ever heard about. Now I'm not one to spread idle gossip or rumor, but she left his staff against her will, that much I know."

Alex said, "I had no idea Rose ever worked for him."

Les nodded. "She was his housekeeper. I guess you were still a boy, you wouldn't have any reason to know, but I heard a rumor that there were accusations of a theft that couldn't be explained away. Rose had a devil's time getting another job, and she holds a grudge to this day.

That's probably why I'm fond of her myself. Partners in sorrow, that kind of thing."

As they drove up Point Road, Les looked at the lighthouse. "That overgrown nightlight of yours is really something, Alex. You think Tracy's going to be able to twist enough arms to get it turned on more than once a year?"

"That was supposed to be a secret. How'd you find out."

Les said, "Folks will say the darnedest things waiting for an appliance to get fixed. I don't think they believe I'm listening half the time. Well, sir, here you are, right to your doorstep."

As Alex got out, he said, "Thanks Les, I appreciate the lift. Do you have time for a cup of coffee?"

He shook his head. "Thanks, but no, I'd better get back to that cream separator before Carole comes looking for me. She's doing her best to live up to the redhead's reputation."

As the elder handyman drove away, Alex marveled that he'd missed the connection between Reston Shay and Rose Lane. He hesitated on the front steps, needing some time to think about it. If she'd been in Reston's employ, why had Rose come out to the inn to see the Carolina Rhapsody? Wouldn't she have had the opportunity to see it at Reston's house? There were rumors that years ago he'd kept it on his desk before getting skittish and moving it to a safety deposit box at the bank. Was Rose the reason he'd become more cautious? Alex was going to have to go to one of his sources in town to get the back story he'd somehow missed. If Les had known more specifics about the accusation, there was no doubt he would have shared them with Alex. He was going to have to see which of his oldest friends might remember what had happened between the housekeeper and her boss.

Elise joined him outside. "I was beginning to wonder if you were ever coming back."

"Why, what's up?"

"Besides the fact that I'm dying of curiosity? Not much. So what did you discover?"

Alex said, "Not nearly as much as I'd hoped. There are prison cells with more personal stuff in them than Cliff's place had."

"Well, in a way that tells us something, too, doesn't it?"

"Whatever it is, it's beyond me. Sorry I was gone so long."

Elise smiled. "You're back just in time. I just finished folding the last clean sheet, and our guests have all checked in. It's time to tackle that lens."

Alex groaned. "Oh no, I forgot all about it."

"Well I didn't," Elise said as she grabbed their buckets and rags from just inside the door. "We're going to start cleaning the lens this afternoon."

"Where'd you find those?" he asked, pointing to the battered old case that held his father's binoculars.

"I was cleaning the attic and found them the other day. We should be able to see the world with them from the upper platform."

He laughed. "Are we working or birdwatching?"

Elise said, "What's wrong with doing a little bit of both?"

Alex followed her up the stairs of the lighthouse, knowing that whatever leads he still had to follow up on would have to wait. Once Elise got something in her mind, there was no stopping her. If there was anyone in the world who wanted Hatteras West to shine more than he did, it had to be his head housekeeper, and also one of his closest friends in the world.

Cleaning the thick glass segments of the elaborate prism lens system of the lighthouse was a massive undertaking, since the Fresnel lens was twelve feet high and six feet in diameter. Twenty-four bull's-eye prism lenses were equally spaced around it, creating a myriad of surfaces in need of attention. It wasn't all that demanding mentally though, and the work gave Alex and Elise a chance to talk.

As Elise worked on one of the lenses, she said, "You need to bring me up to date on what you found at Cliff's apartment."

"Like I said, it was meticulous. The only thing I saw out of the ordinary was lots of books and a few photographs."

"Do you remember any of the titles?"

"Exciting stuff like *Modern Gemology* and *Tectonic Plate Formations*."

Elise said, "So he was a rockhound like a lot of folks around here. Tell me about the pictures."

As Alex worked on a particularly tough spot of haze, he said, "There was one interesting thing about them. A couple of shots had been altered. Somebody took a razor and cut out one of the people posing."

"Sounds like a relationship gone sour. What were the backgrounds of, do you remember?"

"One was on a lake, another was in the mountains. Now I remember, there was one that had been taken in front of a sign that said Mount McKinley."

"So Cliff liked to travel," Elise said. "Funny, he didn't strike me the type."

"I've got a feeling there's a lot we don't know about the man. Armstrong said there was an ex-wife somewhere, but he hadn't been able to track her down."

"How recently did she become his ex?" Elise asked.

"According to the sheriff, it's been years. I can't imagine anybody holding a grudge that long."

"I don't know, you might be surprised. So who else had a reason to kill him?"

"Anybody greedy enough to go after the emerald. The theft itself had to be planned ahead of time, since he had a replica made and ready to use."

Elise said, "Let's make a list of the folks around the inn that day. There might be something we're missing."

"Reston Shay was here," Alex said simply. "We've already discussed the possibility that he might steal the stone, collect the insurance, and still get to keep it."

Elise said, "Skip was here, along with the other guards, but I can't imagine them doing it. They had to alibi each other."

Alex said, "Fiona White was here peddling her muffins, Patrick Thornton was here, and so was Claudia Post. I'd still like to know what was in Thornton's tube. I'm kicking myself for not opening it when I had the chance."

"Don't forget, Claudia Post told you that she'd seen Monet at the inn that day. Rose Lane was out here too, remember? Cliff had to warn her to stay away from the emerald. She could have been getting a closer look to see if her fake matched the real thing."

Alex told her about Rose Lane's animosity toward Reston Shay, and added, "So she could have stolen the gem out of spite, but I can't see her killing Cliff. For that matter, it could have been any of the guests we had staying with us at the time, including Melva. Whoever did it could have dashed back upstairs just as easily as running out the door."

Elise shrugged. "I'm more confused than I was before."

"We need more information. I just wish I knew how to go about uncovering it," Alex said.

Elise paused a moment and turned to look out at the world instead of focusing inside the lighthouse. "Wow, I forgot how beautiful it was up here at the very top." She took out the binoculars and scanned the horizon as she spoke.

"Not many folks get the opportunity to see the mountains from this perspective." They were well above the first balcony at the pinnacle of the lighthouse, and the view was one Alex never grew tired of. As a young boy, he could remember climbing the lighthouse at night with his sleeping bag, a flashlight, and a book, camping out there and gazing out at the world from his very own aerie.

Elise lowered the binoculars and said, "You know, we probably should be getting back. There's more lens surface here than I remembered, and there's no way we're going to be able to finish it this evening."

Alex agreed. "It's pretty massive, isn't it? Why don't we break the job up over several days? That way we have a perfect excuse to come up here and get away from the world."

Elise said, "The world is never all that far away, is it? Do you ever regret having such a demanding job?"

As they gathered their supplies and started the climb back down, Alex said, "It's the only way of life I know. I have to admit, I'm tempted by Harry's offer. It would be great staying in a lighthouse located on an actual body of water."

"It would certainly be different," Elise said. "Have you really thought any more about it?"

He said, "I wanted to talk to you a little more before I call Harry. It's kind of presumptuous of me to assume you'll do whatever I choose."

Elise said, "Come on, I think it would be fun. We should absolutely do it."

Down at the base of the lighthouse, Alex opened the door, stepping aside so Elise could pass through first.

As he did, a bullet thudded into the wood of the doorframe.

Someone was shooting at them!

15

Alex grabbed Elise and pulled her back inside the base, then slammed the doors shut.

"What happened?" she asked breathlessly.

"Unless I miss my guess, whoever shot Vince is having a little more target practice."

"That's crazy. Why would anybody shoot at us?"

"Maybe we're closer to the killer than we think," Alex said as he deadbolted the doors. As long as they stayed inside, they should be safe, but how long could they remain holed up in the lighthouse? Sooner or later they had to come out, and if the shooter was still there, it would be the easiest thing in the world to pick them off as they left.

They could be in for a long wait.

"This is one time I regret not having a cell phone," Alex said.

"Don't worry, we're safe enough in here. I just wish I knew why they were shooting at us."

"It would help, wouldn't it?"

Alex headed back up the stairs. Elise asked, "Where are you going?"

"I'm going to look out the window on the first landing. Maybe I can see who's after us."

She grabbed his arm. "That's also a good way to get shot. Don't you think the shooter's watching the windows, too?"

"I'll be careful," Alex said.

Alex peered out through the first window. It was lucky the windows lined up with the doors below. With any luck, he could spot the shooter without being seen. Carefully, he edged toward the opening. As he leaned closer so he could see better, Elise grabbed his arm and pulled him back. A split second later, the glass shattered as the bullet crashed through.

"That was too close," Alex said, feeling his legs shake at the idea of how near a miss it had been. "Thanks."

"Now will you come back downstairs?" Elise asked.

"You've convinced me," Alex said.

Just then, Alex heard a car coming up Point Road toward the lighthouse. He had to alert whoever was coming that there was a shooter loose at Hatteras West.

"What are you doing now?" Elise asked.

"I have to warn whoever's coming," Alex said.

"And get shot at again?"

"I have to take that chance." Alex got close to the window again, being careful to keep out of the shooter's line of sight. As he heard a car door slam, he shouted, "Go back. Somebody's shooting at us."

Armstrong called from below, "Alex, is that you?"

"Sheriff, somebody on the property has a gun."

He couldn't see the sheriff from where he stood, but he heard the man scramble back to his car and slam the door.

After a minute, Alex heard him call, "Hold on, I've got my men on their way."

Less than ninety seconds later the first squad car came, and in ten minutes all four of Elkton Falls's patrol cars were parked in front of the inn. Fifteen minutes after that,

Armstrong called out, "Alex, it's all clear. You can come out now."

Alex unbolted the doors, and he and Elise stepped outside. He asked, "Did you catch them?"

"No, whoever it was got away clean. We've got one bullet lodged in your doorframe, if we ever get anything to match it to."

"There's one inside the lighthouse, too. If we could find the one that shot Vince, I've got a feeling all three will match."

"You need to be careful, Alex. Somebody's got it in for you. Are you all right, Elise?"

"I'm fine now. So what are you going to do about this?"

Armstrong shrugged. "I'll step up the patrols out here, but I can't tie everybody up without more to go on. Chances are whoever took those shots at you is long gone."

Alex shook his head. "It just doesn't make sense. Why would somebody shoot at us?"

"There are a lot of nutcases in the world, Alex. You'll go crazy if you try to figure them out."

Elise said, "Sheriff, why were you coming out here in the first place?"

Armstrong said, "I hate to mention it now. It doesn't seem all that important."

Alex said, "Well, you're here. What's going on?"

Armstrong said, "My church is having a cake sale to raise money for foreign missions, and I was kind of hoping Elise could make something for it. She's the best baker around."

Elise laughed, as much from the release in tension as the odd request. "Sheriff, I'd be delighted. While you're at it, you should ask Fiona White for a donation."

Armstrong said, "The Muffin Lady? I already asked her. She only does muffins, can you believe that? It's hard to believe there's enough business around Elkton Falls for that."

"She probably works Hickory, Bethlehem, Granite Falls, and Hudson, too. She might even go all the way to Lenoir."

"That's still not a big territory, not when you're talking about muffins. Listen, if you two see anything suspicious, and I mean anything at all, I want you to call me, day or night, you hear?"

"We will," Alex said.

Armstrong nodded. "Good enough. I'm sending Irene out later to collect that bullet. I'm afraid she's going to have to chop up that frame a little to get it out in one piece."

Alex groaned at the thought of the lighthouse being attacked yet again. "Just tell her to be careful, would you? I'm going to have a tough enough time patching it up as it is."

"You know Irene, she'll do what she has to do. In the meantime, you ought to get that glass fixed."

"That I can do myself. I've got some glass stored in the shed."

Armstrong patted Alex's shoulder. "Be careful now, you hear?"

"I'll do my best," Alex said. As the patrolmen peeled off and went back to their duties, the sheriff followed close behind.

Alex scanned the trees around the inn, trying to see where the shooter had hidden, but he didn't have any more luck than the sheriff and his men had.

Elise asked, "Alex, could we go inside?"

He nodded. "I feel it, too. It's as if someone was watching us, isn't it?"

Elise shivered noticeably. "I just hope they catch them soon."

"Until then, we both need to be on our guard, and that

means no more lens cleaning until this lunatic is caught. Agreed? We can't take any more chances."

Elise said, "Hey, I'm not the one snooping around a murder. I'll promise to be careful if you do."

"I'm always careful," he said.

"You know what I mean."

Alex nodded. "I'll watch my step."

Melva came downstairs as they were closing the lobby door behind them. "What was all that commotion about? I saw a dozen police cars out front."

Alex knew Elkton Falls would have to borrow eight cars to make a dozen, but he let that slide. "Somebody was careless with a gun," he said.

Melva said, "You certainly run a more interesting place than I imagined. Did you happen to get any more of those postcards in?"

Elise handed her another stack, and Melva took them and headed back to her room.

"I can't even imagine what she's going to write tonight," Elise said.

"I've got a feeling this installment will be more suspense than romance."

"Should we warn all our guests to be careful?" Elise asked. Neither one of them wanted to consider the possibility of shutting the inn down until the shooter was found, but it was obvious the prospect was in both their minds.

"We owe them that, and the chance to leave if they want without penalty. I don't like having my guests in jeopardy."

"I know. Oh Alex, just when we get things going again, something like this seems to happen."

"Do you believe in family curses? You know, some folks believe the lighthouse is haunted."

"Well I'm not one of them," she said. "We'll get through this."

"With you here, I actually believe it," Alex said.

"So what do we do now?"

"After we talk to our guests, I'm going into town. There are a few folks there I want to have a word with."

"Anybody in particular?" Elise asked.

"I'd like to know if anybody's bought a rifle or ammunition recently, and Shantara's the only one nearby who sells either one of them. While I'm in town, I'd like to snoop around and find out more about Cliff and Reston Shay."

"Promise you'll be careful," Elise said again.

"Don't worry about me. After I'm gone, I think you should stay inside the inn, and if you can manage it, keep away from the windows."

"I won't go outside, but I won't let this maniac keep me penned up in my room either."

"I guess that's the best I can hope for, isn't it?"

"You're lucky I agreed to that," Elise said, her smile flickering for just a moment before disappearing again.

"Don't worry, I won't be long," Alex said.

"I'm counting on it," Elise said.

Surprisingly, none of their guests decided to leave Hatteras West. Alex was gratified to get the business, he needed every visitor they had, but as he drove into Elkton Falls, he couldn't help worrying that he'd downplayed the shooting to the point where no one was taking his warning seriously enough. The Hatteras West Inn didn't need to add to its list of casualties, and if Alex could do anything about it, it wouldn't.

Shantara Robinson was helping a man with the oddest accent Alex had ever heard in Elkton Falls. After he was gone, Shantara said, "He's from Wales, can you imagine him stumbling into my store?"

"How did he find you?" Alex asked.

Shantara said, "My advertising goes all over the world."

When she saw Alex wasn't buying it, she added, "Actually, he was looking for Blowing Rock."

"I hope you set him straight," Alex said.

"Absolutely, right after he bought some of Bill Yadkin's ironwork. Have you seen his latest stuff? The man's getting really good."

"I'm glad he's having some success. Speaking of Bill, have you seen Rachel Seabock around?" The two had been dating since just before the Golden Days Fair at Hatteras West.

Shantara smiled. "Absolutely, she comes by all the time. In fact, she just brought in the coolest chair." After she showed it to Alex, Shantara said, "Last I heard they were still going out together. What brings you into town this late in the day?"

"You haven't heard yet? The kudzu vine must be broken. Somebody took a shot at Elise and me in the lighthouse. Two shots, actually."

"Is she all right?"

"Thanks for your concern about me," Alex said.

"You obviously didn't get hit, not anywhere that counts, anyway."

He said, "Elise is fine. We were more scared than anything else, but that's why I'm here. Have you sold any rifles or ammunition lately?"

"You're kidding, right? Hunting season's getting ready to start, everybody's been stocking up."

"Could I see your records?"

Shantara said, "I can't do that, not with all the confidentiality stuff we have to promise to do in order to keep our license. Hang on a second, would you?"

Shantara walked to her office, one even smaller than Alex's, got a folder out of her filing cabinet and laid it on her desk. When she rejoined him, a customer walked in. "Could you wait in my office? I should be about five minutes."

"I don't mind waiting out here," Alex said. "That way I can look around."

"You really should wait in my office," Shantara insisted.

Alex said, "Sure, sorry, didn't mean to get in your way."

He felt like a nitwit when he saw the folder on her desk. It was a list of all the folks who had bought guns and ammo from her in the past two weeks.

After looking through the folder, Alex saw that Shantara was right. It seemed as though half the town had bought supplies for hunting season, including several women. Skip's name was there, and so was Rose Lane's, along with Sheriff Armstrong, David Daroo, who was the minister of the Baptist Church and Doc Drake's name as well.

It looked like another dead end.

Alex closed the folder and found Shantara dusting some jars of pumpkin butter. "I forgot you were here," she said, grinning slightly as she studied him. "Now what were you asking me before?"

"I forgot," Alex said. "It must not have been all that important."

"Sorry I couldn't help," she said.

"Thanks," Alex said as he walked out. It was time to gather more information, if he could, on some of the people from Elkton Falls involved in what had happened at the inn. And to do that, Alex knew the source he needed to tap.

He just hoped the bookstore owner was in.

He found Hannah Parsons nestled into one of the overstuffed chairs in her bookstore, lost in a copy of Carolyn Hart's *Death on Demand*. It was an appropriate choice, given that the mystery centered around a bookstore. Though the woman was well into her eighties, Hannah was as fit and spry as anyone Alex knew, and there was always a happy smile on her face.

"Alex, I'm surprised to see you here. You've had some excitement out your way, haven't you?"

"Word spreads fast," Alex said.

Hannah smiled. "One of the sheriff's deputies loves romance novels, he told me about it a few minutes ago. I'm so glad you and Elise are all right. Did they catch the ruffian behind it?"

"Not yet," Alex said. "Do you mind if I ask you about a few folks in town?"

"Well, Alex, you know I'm not one to gossip, but I'd gladly help in any way I can."

"What do you know about Reston Shay? I mean besides all the stuff that's public knowledge."

"Behind the scenes information, is that what you're looking for? Let's see, some folks say he cheated his way into his fortune, but don't you believe it, he inherited every dime of it. There was a scandal thirty years ago about one of his maids, but that's about it, if you discount the crazy stunts he's pulled in the meantime. I got one of those flyers he was handing out for his birthday party in the park. You know that story, don't you?"

"I remember." Alex knew the bookstore owner could make the tale last half an hour, and he didn't have the time. "The scandal with the maid, was that because of theft, by any chance?"

Hannah shook her head. "Nobody in their right mind would steal from Reston Shay, he's got a mean temperament. No, I'm talking about the maid he fired for not returning his affections. He could tell any story he wanted to, but folks around here knew better."

"What was the maid's name? Is she still in town?"

"Oh yes, she never left Elkton Falls. I'm surprised you didn't hear about it, but you were just a kid back then, weren't you? I thought Rose was going to kill him when he dismissed her."

"Rose Lane?" Alex asked.

"None other. What's wrong, Alex?"

"Nothing," he said, trying to hide his excitement. If Rose had that kind of motivation to hate Reston Shay, which it sounded like she did, she might decide to ruin him by stealing the Carolina Rhapsody emerald. But could she kill Cliff? And did she hold a grudge for that long? Alex needed to talk to Rose herself and get a handle on how she still felt. Les's story about Rose's dismissal didn't match the boodstore owner's, and Alex found himself wondering which version, if either, was the true one.

Alex had one more question for the bookstore owner. "Did you know Cliff Cliff very well?"

"Our paths crossed a time or two, but I can't say I cared for him."

"Why was that?" Alex asked.

"I hate to speak ill of the dead, but the man was always looking for an angle, some way to get rich quick, and if it came at somebody else's expense, that didn't seem to trouble him one bit."

That was startling news. No one Alex had talked to had had anything bad to say about the guard. "Was there any incident in particular you had in mind?"

"The last fire chief told me there was never any way to prove it, but he was certain the man burned down his family homestead for the insurance four years ago, and it just so happened to be two days *after* his divorce was final."

"That could have been a coincidence," Alex said.

"The chief said he couldn't prove it, but that fire was deliberate. The house had been on the market almost a year, but nobody wanted it, at least not in the condition it was in. The way I heard it, Cliff convinced his ex-wife would never sell, got her to sign off on it for a tenth of its value, then before the ink was dry he torched the place. She was as mad as a wet cat."

"Whatever happened to her?" Alex asked.

"I never met her. This all happened across the border in Salem Mountain. I wish I knew more."

"Thanks, Hannah, you've been a big help."

"Any time, Alex."

Alex left the bookstore in search of Rose Lane. He had to know if the incident with Reston Shay was still driving her, even after all these years, and if she had it in her to commit murder to get back at him. Alex knew he didn't have any way of telling for sure if she was lying, but he trusted his gut. He thought about getting the sheriff before he talked to the woman, especially since her name had been on that ammunition purchasing list in Shantara's store, but if he kept his questions light enough, he should be fine.

Or so he hoped.

16

It didn't help his confidence level that she was cleaning her rifle when she let Alex into her home, a small cottage barely big enough for one person.

"I didn't mean to interrupt," Alex said.

"Just getting ready for hunting season," she said. "I see that look in your eyes. You think it's crazy for a woman to be out in the woods? I get my buck every year, just like my mamma did, and her mamma before her. There's nothing like the taste of fresh venison."

Alex had never been a fan of hunting, but he knew that for many of his neighbors, it was a way of life. He posted the land around the lighthouse inn when hunting season approached every year, and folks knew to pass over his land. There were no grudges or hard feelings though, since Alex's guests usually ended up spending money in town and the last thing they wanted was to drive them away. But the shots were never that far off, and Alex always breathed a sigh of relief when the season was over for another year and none of his guests were among the fatalities.

"Did you change your mind about the job?" Rose

asked. "Sorry you wasted a trip, but I don't want to work there anymore."

"May I ask why?"

"Too many steps, and I'm getting too old."

Alex wondered about the feeble excuse. After all, if the woman was vigorous enough to go traipsing in the woods with a heavy rifle, and carrying back a buck, she could surely handle a few steps at Hatteras West.

"That's not why I'm here," Alex said. "Do you have a minute? I wanted to talk to you about Reston Shay."

"What about him?" Rose said tightly.

"I understand you used to work for him, but I've heard a couple of different reasons why you left."

"Awful nosy, aren't you?" Rose said as she held the rifle up, pretending to study the sight a foot from Alex's nose.

He said, "It happened a long time ago. I figured nobody ever gave you a chance to tell your side of the story."

"That's water long under that bridge, there's nothing left to talk about, and nobody left to care. If that's why you're here, I've got work to do."

Alex decided to push his luck a little more. "How do you feel about Reston Shay now?"

"Are you asking me if I was happy somebody stole something he loved from him? Oh yes, you can believe that, but I take no joy in that guard getting himself killed, and that's all I have to say."

Alex had pushed hard enough, at least while his subject was holding a rifle in her hands, one she evidently knew how to use. But the interview had left him more confused than ever about whether Rose Lane had had anything to do with what happened at the inn.

Alex would have loved to speak with Cliff's ex-wife, to see if she had been trying to get even with her ex-husband for the money he'd cheated her out of, but without the sheriff's resources, he had no way of tracking her down.

That was one task he was going to have to leave to local law enforcement.

In the meantime, he'd left Elise alone long enough.

It was time to get back to the inn. He should have insisted that Armstrong leave at least one of his patrolmen at Hatteras West, or, at the very least, Alex should have asked Skip or Mor to keep an eye on things. He had to start being more cautious when it came to dealing with the dangers to his guests at the inn, and more critically, to Elise. Her welfare was becoming more and more important to him every day. Alex honestly didn't know what he would do without her, and it had nothing to do with running the inn. As he raced back to Hatteras West, there was a sense of dread growing in the pit of his stomach, an ominous feeling that something had happened to Elise at the inn while he'd been off playing amateur detective. And if it had, he'd never be able to forgive himself.

Alex burst in through the front door. He skidded to a stop as he saw that his fears had been groundless; Elise was safe enough, sitting on the couch by the fireplace talking to Skip.

His fear must have shown on his face. "Alex, what's wrong?" she asked.

"Nothing but my overactive imagination. What's happening?"

Skip shook his head. The former police detective said, "We were just discussing the second shooting. It seems kind of odd that somebody would take a shot at you inside the lighthouse."

"I can't figure out why they'd do it, either," Alex said. "We're no closer to coming up with an answer to this mess than the sheriff is."

Elise said, "That's not what he means. Why didn't the shooter just wait until we were far enough outside, instead of taking his chances while we were still so close to safety?"

"I don't know, maybe he rushed his shot," Alex said as he sat beside Elise. Just her presence gave him a warm buzz that replaced the dread he'd felt so recently.

Skip said, "I guess it could be that, but I doubt it. Here's what I think. Those shots were a warning. Otherwise, you'd both be dead."

The finality of the tone in his voice sent a chill through Alex's heart. If things had gone just a little differently, one or both of them wouldn't be sitting there.

"Alex, are you all right?" Elise asked, putting her hand lightly on his arm.

He returned the touch, and he was pleased to see that she didn't pull away. "I will be."

Skip, aware that they were having a moment, said, "Well, if you'll excuse me, I want to look around a little more."

"It's getting pretty dark out there," Alex said.

"Perfect for cover, wouldn't you say? I haven't done a stakeout in a long time. Would you mind if I watched the inn tonight, just for my satisfaction?"

Alex said, "That's a great idea. I'll put you on the pay-roll." He added, "I'm not sure what you charge, but I'll pay it willingly tonight."

Skip said, "I'm not opening a business, Alex, this is just something I want to do."

"And paying you is something I want to do," Alex said. He could be just as stubborn as the ex-cop, if it came to that.

Elise said, "Why don't we discuss payment later? Skip, if you're not interested in money, how about a free night's stay at the inn for you or anyone else you'd like to give it to. Is that more to your liking?"

"My sister *has* been talking about coming up to visit me. She lives in Georgia."

"Then it's settled," Elise said. "I'll go get you a thermos of coffee. Is there anything else you'd like?"

"I wouldn't say no to a sandwich or two," Skip admitted.

"Say no more, it's coming right up."

After Elise went off to make the care package, Skip said, "She's something, isn't she?"

"I've known it from the start," Alex agreed.

Skip stood up and walked around the lobby. "She loves this place as much as you do. That's got to be a rare find in an employee."

"She's a lot more than that to me," Alex said.

Skip grinned. "I knew that. I just wasn't sure you did."

"I'm not the one who's the problem," Alex said after returning the smile with one of his own.

Skip laid a hand on Alex's shoulder. "Well, take some advice from an old man. That lady is worth the effort."

"You're preaching to the choir," Alex said as Elise rejoined them, a picnic basket in her hands.

"About what?" she asked as she handed the care package to Skip.

"Nothing," Alex said hastily.

Skip added, "Thanks for doing this. I appreciate it."

Elise retrieved a throw from one of the couches, one emblazoned with different lighthouses around the country. "You'd better take this, it's going to get chilly tonight."

"I can't get too comfortable," he said as he took the blanket. "Thanks again."

"You're very welcome."

After Skip was gone, Alex asked, "How's everything going here?"

"Just dandy. It's kind of quiet, even though we have nearly a full house."

"So we don't have any late-nighters in the group," Alex said. Usually there was at least one guest who kept night owl hours, staying up late and rising sometime around noon, but for once they had the lobby to themselves.

Elise said, "Give them time, it's early yet."

"How about a fire?" Alex suggested.

"That would be lovely," Elise agreed, and Alex lit the kindling he kept there, always ready for the next excuse to light a fire.

"That's nice," Elise said as she settled onto one of the couches. Instead of taking his usual seat across from her, Alex joined her there.

"Alex Winston, what are you up to?"

"Elise, there's nothing like getting shot at to clear your head. You know what I kept thinking when we were pinned down inside the lighthouse?"

"That we weren't going to make it," she said in a soft voice that was barely above a whisper.

"Not just that. I kept thinking how much time we've wasted since we've met. I don't want to waste any more," he said as he leaned forward to kiss her. Even if she pulled away before he could kiss her, he owed himself the attempt.

To his surprise, Elise didn't pull back at all. They melted together as if they'd been coupled all their lives. After a few seconds, though, she broke away from him.

"Alex. We shouldn't."

"Why not, Elise?" Alex said. "We're both consenting adults here."

"I still don't think it's a good idea."

Alex said, "Come on, you have to admit you have feelings for me too. You can't hide that."

Elise said, "I'm not trying to hide anything. I feel something for you, I won't deny it. But Alex, if we tried to have a relationship, it could ruin everything. If it didn't work out, I couldn't bear to stay at Hatteras West. I don't give my heart lightly, but once I do, it's a commitment I make with everything I've got. That's why I was so reluctant to end it with Peter."

Alex knew full well what a difficult time Elise had had ending her engagement to Peter Ashford.

"I'm not asking you to marry me," Alex said, though the prospect wasn't exactly out of the question. "I do think that if we let this opportunity pass us by, it might be our last chance of ever being together."

"Alex, I'm not going anywhere. You know how much I love Hatteras West."

Alex took a deep breath. "You'll always be welcome here, I couldn't run this place without you, I hope you know that. I'm not talking about work right now, Elise. I've made no secret about how I feel about you for a long time." She started to speak, but he held his hand up. "Let me finish or I may never have the courage again. If you honestly aren't interested in being with me, I'm going to have to do my best to forget about my feelings for you, and the only way I can do that is to move on. I don't want to, believe me, you are the only woman I want to be with, but my heart can't take this anymore, at least not the way things stand now." He felt himself shaking after the declaration, but he knew in his deepest core that it was true. Having Elise there with him every day, working side by side, holding out hope that someday they could be together, was slowly destroying him if it could never be. He was so lost in her he wasn't sure he'd be able to pull himself back if she didn't, or wouldn't, return his love.

"I don't know what to say," Elise said.

"I'm not putting pressure on you," Alex said, "but it's something you need to think about." He took her hands in his. "Elise, it's okay to be afraid, I'm scared myself, but no matter what happens, I believe in my heart we can work things out between us. But we both have to want it, and we both have to be willing to give it a chance. Otherwise, it will never work."

She stood, pulling her hands from his. "I won't keep you dangling any longer than I can help. Give me a few days to think about what you've said."

"I hope I haven't scared you off," Alex said as she started for her room.

"No, I don't blame you a bit for what you said." She lingered before going through her door. "Alex?"

"Yes?"

"Know that no matter what happens, I do care about you."

He smiled gently. "I know that. I care about you, too."

"Good night."

"Good night," he said as she disappeared. Had he blown it with her forever, or was his ultimatum the shove she needed into his arms? Time would tell which would be the result, but one thing was certain. Soon enough a new chapter would be starting in his life, one with Elise by his side, or one where he renewed his search for someone to spend the rest of his life with.

And suddenly nothing else seemed all that important to him anymore.

17

Alex woke up the next day, glad the miserable night was finally over. A small part of him wouldn't let go of the possibility that he'd blown any chance of ever having a relationship with Elise outside the Hatteras West Inn. He was still glad he'd done something at last about the frustrating situation between them, but his conviction wasn't one hundred percent certainty, not by any means. Steeling himself with a quick icy shower and a brisk toweling, he couldn't delay his room exit any longer. It was time to go to the lobby and see if his fate had been determined yet.

Alex wasn't sure what he was expecting from Elise when he came out into the lobby. Oddly enough, she wasn't there yet, though she usually beat him by at least half an hour. Neither batch of muffins for the day had arrived yet, either. That was the first thing he checked. Alex glanced at the clock. It was barely past six A.M., so they weren't due for another forty-five minutes. He busied himself by brewing a fresh pot of coffee, laying out the fruit, and setting up their light buffet. After that was accomplished, there was nothing more he could do for the moment, so Alex cleaned out the ashes from the previous night's fire and started preparing things for the next time.

Elise came in as he placed the last log. "What a grand idea, a fire in the morning. There is a nip in the air, isn't there?"

Alex was relieved to see her smile. There was no awkwardness in her voice, but there was no added warmth there, either. "My thought exactly," he said, which was a total lie. Alex struck one of the long matches and the fatwood kindling jumped to life. Soon they were greeted by the aroma and warmth of the fire, and Alex realized it was a custom he could grow to like.

"I need to talk to Wilbur McFear," Alex said. "At the rate we're burning wood around here, we're going to need more firewood than I ordered."

Elise said reluctantly, "I suppose we could cut back."

"No way, I love it as much as the guests do. Besides, Wilbur lives for cutting wood. He'll be delighted, he's been after me for years to double my order."

"He's kind of an odd bird, isn't he?" Elise asked.

"For Elkton Falls? I think he fits right in."

"Is it true he taught at Harvard, and now he lives in a shack and cuts firewood?"

Alex said, "I don't know how these rumors get started. He never taught at Harvard, though he was a guest lecturer on economics at Stanford a time or two in the sixties. Wilbur took his economics know-how and invested it wisely enough in the stock market to retire at forty. He told me once that he'd had enough of the outside world, sold everything he had in the market, then bought a chainsaw and two hundred acres of forest. He's been happy ever since thinning his stands and selling the firewood. I wouldn't call his place a shack either, it's cozy enough for one man, and he told me he was afraid if he built anything bigger people would be more inclined to visit."

"You know what I want more than just about anything?"

"I'd love to hear it," Alex said.

"I'd like to be just another story around Elkton Falls. You've made that status yourself, you know."

Alex was surprised by the statement. "How's that? I'm one of the most ordinary guys you'll ever meet."

Elise smiled at that. "If you count men who own lighthouses in the mountains and run them as inns, you're as common as a penny."

Alex laughed. "Sometimes I forget that most lighthouses aren't as landlocked as mine is. It's just always been here." He glanced at the clock. "Where's Fiona, anyway? She's running late again and Sally Anne's behind, too."

"I know. The last few days Fiona's grown a little too complacent for my taste. I'll speak with her."

They heard a knock outside and Fiona White herself was there, laden with a big basket of muffins. "Sorry I'm late," she said with a sing-song voice. "The sunrise reminded me of a time I was at Denali in the springtime. Beautiful country." She shook herself gently, then said, "Tell you what, I'll throw in an extra muffin on the house to atone for my tardiness."

"We need them here when the guests come down for breakfast," Elise said gently.

Fiona glanced at the clock and said, "I've a minute to spare then; Alex told me you don't start serving until a quarter till seven."

Though that was the true starting time listed at the inn, Alex and Elise were used to having the fare out and ready by six thirty at the latest. Their guests seemed to appreciate it, as it gave them an early start on their day trips into the mountains.

Elise was about to say something else when Patrick

Thornton came downstairs. He said sternly, "Alex, I need to speak with you."

"Certainly," Alex said. There were a few things he'd like to cover with the surveyor himself.

"Let me grab some coffee and we can go in your office," Thornton said.

"Wouldn't you care for a muffin, as well?" Fiona asked, offering the basket toward him.

"No thanks, I don't care for them," he said.

Fiona's smile vanished for a moment, and Alex could see Elise fighting back her laughter. It was good seeing her back to her old self, but he couldn't help wondering if she'd made her decision, and worse yet, if it was one he wasn't going to like hearing.

Patrick tapped his shoulder. "I'm ready if you are."

Alex nodded to Elise and Fiona, then followed Patrick into his tiny office. Alex sat behind the desk and said, "What can I do for you?"

"You can stop meddling in my room, for one thing," the surveyor said abruptly.

"I'm not sure I know what you mean," Alex said, somewhat taken aback by the directness of the man's comments.

"Let's stop with the games, shall we? I know you found my hiding place in the toilet. I carefully marked the location before I placed my packet there, and when I returned it had been moved."

Alex thought about playing dumb, but he wouldn't learn anything that way. "Your toilet kept running; I noticed it while I was cleaning your room. It's my job to keep things in good repair around here, so I lifted off the reservoir lid and found your little tube blocking the stopper. I wasn't going to bring it up, but since you've seen fit to mention it, I need to say this. We won't tolerate illegal activities at Hatteras West."

"What in blazes are you talking about?" Thornton asked, tensed on the edge of his chair.

"If you choose to do anything against the law that's your business, but I won't knowingly have it at Hatteras West."

Alex was prepared for more outrage, but Thornton's reaction surprised him. The man started laughing so hard he nearly spilled the cup of coffee in his lap. "Is that what you think? That I've been hiding drugs or something? Let me assure you, Alex, I've never done any such thing in my life."

"Don't try to tell me you were hiding something innocent in there, because I don't believe it."

Thornton said, "Believe what you like. My precautions were for hiding a sum of money I owed my ex-wife. She demanded her alimony payment in cash this month, and yesterday she met me in town at that diner of yours."

"We have a safe here at the inn, you know," Alex said. "You would have been free to use it."

"Pardon me for saying so, but some of the safes I've seen in small towns aren't as secure as I'd like. I've taken to storing my valuables in my room whenever I'm away." He finished his coffee, then said, "I'm glad we cleared that up, aren't you?"

"I suppose," Alex said, still not believing the surveyor's story entirely. "Will you be checking out this afternoon, Mr. Thornton?"

"I thought we agreed I'd keep the room until my work is finished here."

"I just assumed you had to be close to wrapping things up," Alex said. "After all, how much more could there be to do around here?"

"Quite a bit, I'm afraid. It appears the original survey was off by substantial yardage. In fact, I'm sorry to say that some of it is going to directly affect you."

That caught Alex's attention. "What are you talking about?"

"I'm not positive, I have more sightings to make and a

few more calculations, but it appears that the property line is much closer to your lighthouse than you think."

"How close?" Alex asked, barely able to breathe.

"As it stands now, the line appears to run right through the center of it."

"You've got to be kidding," Alex said, his face suddenly gone numb.

"I'm afraid it's looking more and more likely. There's no need to panic at this point, but I wouldn't count on things staying the way they are."

"I'm calling my attorney," Alex said. "She'll know how to handle this."

As he reached for the telephone, Thornton put a hand on the receiver. "That's premature, let me assure you. There's no need to get an attorney involved until I make my formal report, and I'm nowhere near doing that now. I haven't even found the one benchmark I need to determine the exact line. That's what's taking me so blasted long here."

"Then why did you tell me it cut right through the lighthouse?"

Thornton said, "I said it might. Give me seven days. By then I'll have an answer for you. Now I've got to go. I've a great deal of work to do today."

After he was gone, Alex thought about what he should do for all of twenty seconds before he called his attorney, Sandra Beckett.

"I hope I didn't wake you," Alex said when Sandra picked up after the seventh ring.

"No, I just got back from my run. This can't be good, you calling me this early. What happened, did you find another body at Hatteras West?"

"I hope I've found my last one. Listen, I've got a surveyor here who claims that my lighthouse might not even be on my property. He told me not to worry about it right now, but I feel like I'm going to lose it."

"Don't worry about anything yet. Let me get into the office and I'll see what I can come up with. Real estate isn't my field, but I've got some friends I can call."

Just knowing Sandra was on top of it made Alex feel better. She was very good at what she did; he'd seen her in court enough to know that.

"Thanks. I appreciate this."

"I'd tell you not to worry, but I won't waste my breath. I'll call you later when I hear something myself."

Alex was just hanging up when Elise came in. "What was that all about?"

"Thornton just dropped a bombshell on me. He said the lighthouse might not be part of my property after all."

"Alex, that's impossible. It's been in your family since it was built."

"I know, but we've been selling off land in bits and pieces for generations. If one of those surveys was wrong, we could lose possession of the lighthouse. Without that, there's no reason to keep running Hatteras West as an inn."

"Let's not borrow trouble. How can we find out for sure what's going on?"

"I just got off the telephone with Sandra, she's going to look into it and get back to me."

Elise said, "I'll give her that, she won't let anyone cheat you. Oh, Alex, I'm so sorry."

"So am I. If Thornton is right about the lighthouse, I don't know what I'm going to do. I don't have enough to buy the true owner out, and I won't own half a lighthouse that's been mine all these years. I don't know, maybe it's time to move on with my life and do something else with it."

"Don't give up yet. You've got to believe."

"The only thing I'm beginning to believe is that I never should have gotten up this morning."

Elise said, "I know what will take your mind off things. Let's go clean the rooms. We can do them together today if we hurry."

"I'll be there in a minute. I want to go check on Skip."

Elise said, "Goodness, I forgot he was still out there. Let me come with you."

Alex said, "I appreciate the offer, but I'd rather do this by myself."

"You're trying to protect me, aren't you? You've got to stop doing that, Alex, I'm a grown woman."

"Believe me, you don't have to keep reminding me," Alex said. "If you want to come, you're more than welcome."

Elise looked a great deal less certain about coming along as she followed Alex out to the parking area. Skip had told them he'd be in the shadows, parked by the storage shed of the lighthouse where he could keep an eye on things. Alex was relieved to see the car still sitting there; the man had stayed true to his word watching over the inn.

But the closer Alex got, the more worried he became. Instead of sitting upright with his gaze on the inn, the body in the car was slumped forward over the wheel.

It appeared that Alex's worst fear had just come true.

18

"You don't want to see this," Alex said, turning to Elise.

"I can handle it," she said, though he heard the quiver in her voice.

"There's no reason for you to have to, but I won't argue with you."

Alex's hand was shaking as he put it on the door handle. There was no sign of trauma, no blood or bullet holes that he could see, but Skip looked as if he'd been dead for some time.

As Alex pulled the door handle open, hoping to check for a pulse he was certain he wouldn't find, he nearly had a heart attack when Skip snorted once, then woke up.

Rubbing his eyes, the ex-cop said, "I can't believe it, I fell asleep on a stakeout. What time is it?"

"It's just after seven. I can't tell you how relieved I am that you're okay."

"What, you thought I was another body? Well I might as well have been. I'm so sorry, Alex, Elise. I don't know what happened."

"No harm done," Elise said. "We're just glad you're not hurt."

Skip said, "Listen, I need to go. I'm truly sorry about what happened."

Before Alex could say another word, Skip drove quickly away.

"Why did he leave so abruptly?" Elise asked. "I was going to have him in for a cup of coffee and a muffin."

"It was pretty obvious, wasn't it? He was embarrassed," Alex said. "He fell asleep on the job."

"It could have happened to anyone," Elise said. "There's nothing to be embarrassed about."

Alex didn't know how to explain to her that in Skip's mind he had put them in mortal jeopardy through his own weakness. It wasn't machismo; it was something much more than that. The one-time detective had failed to deliver on a promise; probably for the first time in his career he'd let down his charge.

"It's a guy thing," Alex said, aware that the explanation was nearly as unsuitable as no answer at all.

As they walked back into the inn, Alex saw that some of his newest guests were already seated and eating. Elise took Alex to their tables and made the introductions. Eve Newton finished her bite of muffin and said, "How do you get these from Charlotte and manage to keep them so fresh?"

"Ma'am?" Alex asked.

"The muffins. They're from Dessert Delights in Charlotte, aren't they? I just adore their baked goods."

Alex said, "No, Ma'am, they're baked by a woman right here in Elkton Falls."

Eve studied the muffin, then said, "She must have worked there at one time, then. The taste and sheer size are unmistakable. Now Mr. Winston, we were quite disappointed the lighthouse wasn't on last night. I trust it will be it tonight."

Alex said, "I wish we could, but we're still waiting for approval from the town council."

Eve turned to her companion, Leah Baker, and said, "Oh, dear, I do hope I didn't get you here on false pretenses. I was certain the lens would be lit every night. Why else have one?"

Leah said softly, "Eve, the tower itself is enough. Are you finished with your muffin yet? I can't wait to see the view from the top. It must be spectacular."

Eve turned to Alex and said, "I trust we're allowed to scale the steps at least."

"I'm not sure that's such a good idea."

Eve said, "Are you telling me it's closed?" There was an edge of anger in her voice. The woman seemed to be one comment away from a tantrum every second of her life.

"I'd just feel better if you didn't take any chances."

Eve said, "Life is full of chances. Come on, Leah."

She looked apologetically at Alex. "We'll be careful, I promise. I do so want to see that view."

Alex nodded. He couldn't very well shut down the lighthouse, especially since it was the main drawing point for his inn. Besides, if what Patrick Thornton had said was true, Alex's guests might not have all that much longer to climb to the top. Whatever legal hassles would be involved in uniting the lighthouse land again would occur after Alex was long gone, though. Losing the Hatteras West light would be the final blow; he wasn't all that certain he could recover from another. It would steal the heart and spirit right from him.

After Leah and Eve were gone, Elise said, "Alex, may I speak with you a moment?"

"Sure thing," Alex said as he joined her at the buffet to grab something for himself. In his haste of the morning he'd neglected to eat anything, and there was no way he could tackle cleaning rooms on an empty stomach. He grabbed a cherry muffin and an orange juice, then followed Elise into his office. As he crossed the threshold, he wondered if she'd made her decision so quickly.

"What's on your mind?" he asked. Suddenly his appetite was completely gone.

"I'm worried about the inn. Do you think you should bring in someone who specializes in property rights? I'm not saying anything bad about Sandra, but she's a trial lawyer. I'm not certain she's who you need."

"Believe me, Sandra knows her limitations. She's looking into this, calling some of her colleagues to get their opinions. It wouldn't surprise me if she had her law school class reunion booklet out and was making calls right now. Until we find out more, there's nothing we can do about it except try to go about our business. Is there anything else I need to know about?"

"Sally Anne called a while ago. She's pulling out of the muffin contest. She said something about understanding, and that there was a fresh peach cobbler waiting for you at Buck's."

"Okay, I understand. Is there anything else you want to talk about?"

Elise hesitated, then said, "No, not yet, but there will be soon, I promise."

"That's all I ask," Alex said. "If it's okay with you," he added, "I think I'll tackle my rooms by myself. I've got a lot to think about."

She nodded and said, "So do I," as she left.

There was a great deal more he wanted to discuss with her, but Alex knew there was no rushing her now. He'd laid his heart out for her one last time. That was all he could do. The rest was up to her.

He took a bite of the muffin as he looked out the window and had just about recovered his composure when he spotted Patrick Thornton walking past, studying a map held in his hands as if it showed the way to the Holy Grail.

All of a sudden Alex didn't have much of an appetite anymore. He threw what was left of the muffin into the trash can, drained the juice, and decided it was time to salvage what he could of his day. If his time as the innkeeper at the Hatteras West Inn was nearing its close, he wanted to be sure he gave it everything he had, to the very end.

Alex knew that Patrick Thornton's room was unoccupied, so he decided to start there first. Though Thornton could be bringing about the end of Alex's life as he knew it, there was no way the innkeeper in him could keep Alex from doing the very best job he could.

After vacuuming the throw rug and sweeping the hardwood floor in the surveyor's room, Alex noticed the edge of something sticking out from under the dresser. It was a rolled up sheet of paper, and at first Alex thought it might be the edge of the tube Thornton had stashed away in his toilet. It wasn't the tube, but it did appear to be something that had been stored in a cylinder. Alex carefully unrolled the sheet, not sure what he was going to find. It turned out to be the oddest thing, a computer printout of an analysis on a sample recently sent to a lab in Raleigh. Alex read down the list of components until one stopped him short. He looked further and read the summary at the end of the analysis. Wherever that test sample had come from, there had been gold present in a large enough quantity to catch anyone's attention. Now why would a surveyor have that in his room? Alex suddenly remembered the gold found in Cliff's pocket. Had it been a lucky talisman, something like Reston Shay's meteorite, or was it somehow tied to the surveyor? Could Patrick Thornton's real reason for being at Hatteras West have something to do with that sheet of paper in Alex's hand? He rolled the sheet back up into a cylinder and put it in his shirt pocket. Alex had let one possible piece of evidence get past him by not opening the tube when he'd found it. There was no way he was going to let something else escape his attention. He raced downstairs, made a copy of the sheet, then hurriedly put the original back where he'd found it.

He considered finding Elise and sharing his latest information with her, but there were rooms to clean yet, and nothing so urgent about the paper that she needed to be told immediately. Besides, he wanted more time to mull over what his latest discovery could mean before he brought it to Elise's attention.

That afternoon they were dusting the Main Keeper's Quarters' lobby when the telephone rang. Since Elise was closest, she picked it up and answered, "Hatteras West Inn."

Alex loved to hear her say it, no matter how many times she repeated the phrase.

Elise frowned slightly, nodded, then said, "I'll get him, he's right here."

She covered the mouthpiece with her hand and said, "It's Sandra. She's got some news for you."

Alex hurried to the phone, wondering if the fate of his inn had already been sealed.

"Hi, Sandra. What did you find?"

"Easy, Alex, I just got started, but I've talked with a few friends of mine, one in Charlotte and the other in Greensboro, and I think you've got a real chance, regardless of what the surveyor finds."

"What do you mean? How is that possible?"

Sandra said, "Hang on a second, let me get my notes. Blast it all, I left them in my briefcase, which happens to be out in the car at the moment. Give me a couple of minutes and I'll call you right back."

"I don't need the legalese, you can paraphrase if you'd like."

Sandra said, "Okay, what it boils down to is there's a case to be made that because you've been maintaining the property as long as you have, with the other owner's apparent knowledge, you've got rights to the land legally."

"So I get my lighthouse and land back by default? No thanks. Sandra, I don't want it that way. If it's not mine by all rights, I don't have a claim to it at all." It killed him to say it, but it was true. He couldn't, in all good conscience, keep anything that didn't belong to him, even if it meant giving up the lighthouse he so loved. By keeping the place on shady moral grounds, the property would be tainted forever for Alex. The problem was, Alex couldn't afford to buy the rest of the lighthouse back; he could barely pay for the inn's day-to-day operation. "Thanks anyway."

Sandra said, "Alex Winston, if you think I'm dropping this, you've clearly lost your mind. I know how much that overgrown nightlight means to you, and if there's any way in the world I can save it for you, I'm going to."

"I do appreciate it, but a loophole's not going to do. If my father or grandfather sold that land in good faith, I'm not going to be the one to break it. Are we clear on that?"

"You're tying my hands, but it's what I expected from you. Sorry I couldn't come up with a slam dunk for you."

"I appreciate you trying," Alex said as he hung up.

Elise had approached and was hanging on every word. "It's hopeless, isn't it?"

Alex touched her shoulder lightly. "Of course not. Sandra said there might be something we can do."

As a tear tracked down Elise's cheek, she said, "I heard you, Alex. You're going to insist on your ancestor's intent, aren't you?"

"It's too soon to start worrying about that now. We've got to get on with our lives."

The telephone rang again and Alex reached for it, happy for the diversion. "Hatteras West," he said, hoping Sandra might have come up with something else.

"Hey, buddy," Mor said.

"Oh, it's you."

Mor laughed. "Well, I've had warmer greetings, I'll tell you that. I hope you drag out a little more enthusiasm for your guests than you do for me."

Alex couldn't help feeling cheered by his friend's happy abuse. "Yeah, well, I'm making an exception for you. What's up?"

"Emma's been dying to use that free dinner offer we all got from Monet before the man gets run out of town."

Alex could hear Emma Sturbridge Pendleton in the background saying, "Mordecai, you tell him the truth. You're the one who's looking for a free meal."

Alex said, "I heard that."

Mor answered, "Yeah, my stomach's been rumbling an awful lot lately."

In the background, Emma said, "Tell him."

Mor covered the phone with a hand, but Alex could still hear him say, "Woman, I'm on the phone here."

Alex shook his head, wondering when the conversation would include him again.

Elise asked, "Who is it?"

He covered the mouthpiece and said, "It's Mor and Emma. They want to go out to Monet's Garden tonight, but I don't think I'm up to it."

"Come on, Alex, we need to do something to cheer us up."

"What about our guests?" he asked.

"They'll be fine without us for a little while. Let's go. It could be fun."

Mor said, "Alex, you still there?"

"Right here," Alex said.

"So what do you say? Are you two interested?"

Alex said, "Okay. Do you want me to call Monet and make the reservation?"

"From what I've heard, it's pretty much deserted, but I'll call him myself to make sure he's got room for us. See you at seven."

After he hung up, Alex said, "They want to eat dinner at seven. Things should quiet down by then. We can hope as much, anyway."

As he spoke, Alex saw Fiona White drive up and slam her car door out in the parking lot. From the angry expression on her face, Alex knew he was in for another gale force assault.

Fiona said, "What's this I've been hearing around town that one of your guests is claiming I stole my muffin recipe from some hack in Charlotte?"

"She wasn't accusing you of anything," Alex said. "She just thought they were remarkably similar."

"If she doesn't have the nerve to say it to my face, she should keep her trap shut," Fiona said harshly.

Elise said, "You're talking about an innocent comment made by one of our guests. I think you're overreacting, Fiona."

The Muffin Lady said, "You do, do you? Nobody's attacking your character, are they?"

"Take it easy," Alex said.

"I won't take it at all, easy or otherwise. A fat lot of support I've gotten from you two. You'd better call Buck's Grill and see if Sally Anne has any more of those rocks she calls muffins for you in the morning."

"You can't do that, we've got an agreement," Elise said.

"Consider it off. I won't sell to a place that stabs me in the back."

"Then we won't pay you," Elise said firmly. "The agreement was that you would supply our muffins till the end of the week, and if you don't make the last delivery in the morning, and by six-thirty at that, you can forget about getting paid."

Fiona stared at Elise for thirty seconds, but Alex knew she was wasting her time. There was no way Elise would back down, not after stating her position so firmly.

"I'll do it, but they're the last muffins you'll ever get from me," Fiona said.

Alex tried to say something to ease the tension, but she stormed off before he could get the words out.

"What do we do now?" Elise asked. "Our guests are expecting muffins every morning as a part of their breakfasts."

"I guess we'd better call Sally Anne and see if she can fit us back in. I don't care how good Fiona's muffins are, I won't have another one at Hatteras West after tomorrow, not with the way she just acted."

Elise nodded. "I couldn't agree with you more. But what are you going to say to Sally Anne?"

"I'm not sure yet, but I imagine there will be some begging and pleading involved."

"I'll talk to her if you'd like. After all, I got us into this mess."

Alex said, "Not without a lot of help from me. Don't worry, it will be fine. Do you still want to go to dinner?"

"Absolutely. I need something to get this bad taste out of my mouth."

Alex asked, "What taste is that?"

"Burnt muffins."

19

"Wow, people are staying away in droves," Mor said as their foursome walked up to the front door of Monet's Garden later that evening. Though it was prime dinner hour, the parking lot was half-empty.

On the drive over, Elise had done her best to fill the time with idle chitchat and speculation, carefully avoiding the one subject Alex wanted to discuss more than anything else in the world. She'd promised him an answer soon, but how soon was obviously relative. It wasn't that he wanted to start dating immediately, but the quicker he found out which direction his life was heading, the better. He could stand losing her, though it would hurt. It was the fact of not knowing where he stood that was killing him. Losing the inn would be another blow, one which he wasn't certain he could ever recover from.

Emma said, "Mor Pendleton, we are here as the owner's guests. I expect you to be civil."

He grinned at her, then said, "I don't suppose there's any harm in expecting it, just as long as you're not mad when it doesn't happen." He pretended to fend off a mock blow as he added, "I'm kidding."

Emma rolled her eyes as she walked ahead, but Alex could see a slight smile peeking through.

When they walked inside, Monet nearly knocked them over with his attention. "So glad to have you with us tonight. I've reserved the best table in the house for you." As he led them to a nice table by one of the expansive windows, Monet said, "I trust this is satisfactory."

Emma fired a preemptive strike before Mor could open his mouth. She said, "It's delightful."

After they were seated, he left them with their new menus and said, "Enjoy."

Mor studied the menu, then said, "Hey, he's come down on his prices."

"And the menu items are mostly different, too," Alex agreed.

Emma said, "But he still has a selection of French cuisine. I believe I'll try the escargot tonight."

Mor said, "Snails? I'm ordering a steak. I just hope it's not charred to a crisp."

Elise said, "I think you'll be pleasantly surprised. His new chef can handle anything on the menu."

Alex explained, "We had lunch here the other day. It was really pretty good." He thought about mentioning that it had been on the house as well, but for once Alex wasn't in the mood to goad his friend.

After they'd placed their orders, Emma said, "Elise Danton, what are you up to?"

She asked, "What do you mean?"

"There's something going on here." She glanced over at Alex, then said, "Is there anything you two would care to share with the rest of us?"

Mor said, "Woman, what are you babbling about?"

Emma retorted, "Shh. Don't interrupt while the grownups are talking."

Alex said, "I guess I'd better be quiet too, then."

Mor nudged him, but didn't say a word.

"Well?" Emma asked again.

Elise said, "I'm sure I have no idea what you're talking about." They had tacitly agreed not to spoil the evening with speculation about the boundary lines until they knew more about where they stood, or mention the ultimatum Alex had given her about their relationship. It was hard keeping secrets from their best friends, but Alex and Elise both knew it was for the best.

When Alex didn't say anything else, Emma said, "It must be my imagination then." Before Mor could say a word, Emma shot him a look that was a clear warning, one that Mor accepted.

"So what's been going on out at the inn? I still can't believe somebody took a shot at you two yesterday," Mor said.

Alex said, "Whoever did it just vanished. Every time I go outside, I can feel a spot the size of a quarter on my chest. I'm pretty shook about this, my friend. I'm afraid to let Elise or any of our guests take a step outside."

Mor said, "Nobody in his right mind can blame you for being concerned." The big man frowned, then said, "Alex, you haven't had me out there in quite a while to fix anything. I'm beginning to think you don't care anymore."

Alex said, "Tell you what, I'll try to break something when we get back."

Mor shook his head. "Hey, I was only kidding. Les has me running around seven counties trying to catch up after our honeymoon." He shot a quick glance at Emma, then added, "Not that it wasn't worth every minute of it."

Emma agreed, then said, "Alex, you really should get away. You haven't left Hatteras West since I've been in Elkton Falls."

Mor said, "He's an innkeeper, Emma. He hasn't left that nightlight of his in donkey years."

Alex looked at Elise, got her nod of approval, then said, "Actually, there's a possibility we might be taking a vacation to the coast later. Sort of a busman's holiday, actually."

"How fun," Emma said after hearing Harry Pickering's proposal.

"It could be," Alex agreed. If he still had an inn to swap, he added softly to himself, and someone to help him run it.

He turned to Emma and said, "I've been meaning to ask you something, since you're our registered gem and precious metal expert."

"No, I'm sorry, I haven't a clue if there are still any emeralds on your land," Emma said. It was one of her responsibilities to be searching for a potential emerald vein somewhere on Winston land, but so far, she'd come up empty.

"I'm not pushing you on that," Alex said. "What I was wondering about is the possibility of gold anywhere around here."

"No, the nearest place I know of is Charlotte. The conditions aren't right around here at all for gold. Why do you ask?"

Alex pulled out the photocopy of the soil analysis paper he'd found in Patrick Thornton's room. He'd meant to tell Elise about it, but he'd been so distracted by her rare talking jag that he hadn't gotten the opportunity on the drive over.

He explained to all of them, "I found this in Patrick Thornton's room."

Elise nodded her acceptance of the fact without accusing him of keeping information from her.

Emma studied the paper, then said, "I don't know where this sample came from, but if I had to say, Alaska would be my first guess."

"What are you talking about?" Mor asked.

Emma explained. "This particular concentration is most likely from Alaska."

"So it's not from around here," Alex asked.

"No, I'd be willing to bet on that, no matter what the header says."

He took the paper back and tucked it into his jacket pocket. If that was true, why had Thornton been hiding it? He'd have to spend some time thinking about that. Thankfully their food arrived and that particular conversation ended.

After they'd finished eating a pleasurable meal, Mor said, "I've got to hand it to the man, that was excellent."

They all agreed. When Monet came to check on them, Alex said, "It was wonderful, but I don't feel right not paying for it."

Monet held his hands up as he said, "Not even the gratuity, my friends. I'm so glad you enjoyed it, and I hope to see you again soon."

"Try to keep us away," Mor said, and Monet's smile brightened.

"I look forward to it."

After they were outside, they decided to split up and call it a night. As Alex and Elise drove back to the inn in the truck, Alex said, "Listen, I meant to tell you about that paper. It just slipped my mind."

"There's nothing to explain," Elise said. "I'm just sorry it was another dead end."

He said, "I've been known to run into one now and then. So, is there anywhere else you'd like to go, or are you ready to go back to Hatteras West?"

"Why don't we go back. We can have a fire and enjoy that. Honestly, I'd rather be at the inn than anywhere else."

"So would I," Alex said. It had become especially true now that he was in real danger of losing it.

There was a message on the machine when they got back to Hatteras West. Oddly enough, it was from Eggars, the man in Florida who owned the orchard that had once belonged to Alex's family before they'd sold it off. And, Alex added, the man who could very well own half of his lighthouse.

"Alex, call me. I don't care what time you get in, we need to talk tonight."

"Who was that?" Elise asked.

"Eggars, the man who owns the orchard."

Elise nodded as Alex dialed the man's number. He picked up on the first ring and said, "Alex?"

"Hi, Mr. Eggars. What's up?"

"Some fool is trying to buy my land, but I keep telling him it's not for sale. What's going on up there?"

Alex said, "Do you know the man's name?"

"He wouldn't say, which made me even more suspicious. I won't do business with a man who won't identify himself, not even if he's waving big money at me."

"You aren't looking to sell, are you?" Alex asked.

Eggars snapped, "Alex Winston, I called you to clear this up, not muddy the waters. What's going on?"

Alex conveyed the surveyor's dire message, only to hear Eggars laugh on the other end of the line.

"What's so funny?" Alex asked, hurt that the old man would find amusement in his sorrow.

"I'm sorry, Alex, but that's the biggest load of manure I've ever heard shoveled. That lighthouse is yours, and all the land around it."

"But he said there was a surveying mistake," Alex said, not trusting himself to believe it was true.

"Oh, there was a mistake, but your fellow up there made it. Alex, I own land in six states, do you think for one second I didn't have that orchard surveyed by a pro before I bought it from your grandfather? There's no possible way a mistake was made."

"Are you sure?" he asked.

"The lighthouse is yours, Alex. You have my word on it. So what's this foolishness all about?"

"I don't know, but I'm going to find out," Alex said.

"Call me when you sort it out. How's the orchard doing?"

"We get enough peaches to keep us in cobbler, and the apples are coming along nicely, too."

"Good, good. I appreciate you looking out for my stake up there."

"Thanks for letting me harvest from it. And thanks for the call, Mr. Eggars. You made my night."

"Glad to help, son."

After they signed off, Alex started toward Patrick Thornton's room. The surveyor had some explaining to do.

Elise grabbed his arm before he could get up the stairs. "Alex Winston, you stop this second and tell me what he said."

"Thornton made a mistake. There's no doubt the lighthouse belongs to me. Eggars is positive, and the man knows what he's talking about."

"So why aren't you celebrating? That's wonderful news."

"It is, but Thornton's not going to think so. Somebody tried to buy the orchard from Eggars, and I've got a sneaking suspicion who it was."

"You mean Thornton was just trying to scare you off so you wouldn't realize what he was up to?"

Alex shook his head. "No, it's worse than that. I think he's the one who tried to kill us."

Elise said, "Alex, how can you be sure?"

"Too many things add up. I seriously doubt he's a surveyor at all, not with the way he's been acting. He's up to no good."

"Then call the sheriff before you confront him," Elise said. "It's not safe to face him alone."

"Do you think Armstrong's going to come out here on

one of my hunches? I can tell you now, it's not going to happen."

Elise put herself in front of him. "You've got to convince him to come out here, Alex. I know you can do it, but if you can't, there's no way I'm going to let you put yourself in danger."

He thought about protesting, but she was right. Alex was in no position to confront the man, not if what he thought was true. "I'll try," Alex agreed.

He found Armstrong at home. "Sheriff, I need you out at Hatteras West."

"You didn't find another body, did you?"

"No," Alex replied, "but I've got an idea who's responsible for shooting at me."

Armstrong said, "Who do you think it was?"

"One of my guests."

The sheriff said, "Alex, it's understandable how all this could shake you up, but now you're pointing fingers at your own guests? What are you basing that on?"

"Would you believe a hunch? I don't have anything concrete. I'm asking you to trust me."

The sheriff took a deep breath, huffed it out, then said, "Alex, I've benefited from a hunch or two of yours in the past. I'll be right there. Don't do anything till I show up."

Alex said, "I won't confront him, but I'm not going to let him walk out of here, either."

"I'm leaving right now," Armstrong said.

Alex grabbed a baseball bat he kept in his room and walked back out into the lobby where Elise was waiting for him. "Alex, you can't go up there by yourself."

He said, "I'm just standing guard. I won't go after him, but he's not leaving the inn."

Elise didn't say a word, but Alex noticed that she kept herself between him and the stairs, just in case he changed his mind. Alex felt calmer than he had in weeks, and it had nothing to do with saving the lighthouse. There was a confidence, even if it was false, that he was finally doing something about the helpless feelings he'd been experiencing.

Armstrong made it up Point Road in record time, and Alex was happy to see that the sheriff had decided against sirens and lights. If they were going to tackle Thornton, it was probably best if the man was unaware of it.

Armstrong came in and asked, "Is he still there?"

"He hasn't gone past me," Alex said. "How do you want to do this?"

"I'm going to knock on his door, tell him it's the police, then we're going to sit down and have a nice long talk."

Alex said, "Why don't you let me knock? I can tell him I have a message for him, that way he won't suspect a thing. When he opens the door, you can go in."

"I don't like you putting yourself at risk," Elise said.

"I'll be fine. He's not expecting anything," Alex said.

Alex knocked on the door of Thornton's room. "Patrick, I've got a message for you."

"Slide it under the door," Thornton said.

"I can't, I'm supposed to deliver it in person."

There was a pause, then Thornton said, "Give me a second, I'm not dressed."

They waited a full minute, and Alex knocked again. "Patrick?"

No answer. "What should we do?" Alex whispered.

"Use your key."

Alex's hand was shaking as he unlocked the door and stepped quickly back. Armstrong went in cautiously, his gun drawn. Then Alex saw the window curtain flapping in the breeze. He heard a car spin out in the gravel outside, then saw a pair of headlights cutting up Point Road.

"He got away," Alex said.

"Not if I can help it."

The sheriff raced out of the room despite his bulk, and

Alex saw his car's headlights quickly follow Thornton's. Alex started to look around the room as Elise joined him.

"I saw him jump off the porch roof, but I couldn't do anything to stop him," Elise said.

"The sheriff will find him. I just hope I was right."

She said, "You had to be. Why else would he run?"

Elise pointed to the bathroom door, partially open. Inside, broken down into its basic pieces, was a rifle that was being cleaned on a bedsheet on the floor. No wonder Thornton hadn't made a stand. His weapon was dismantled, completely apart, and he hadn't had the time to put it back together. It was their luck that they had tackled the man at precisely the right moment.

Armstrong came back a few minutes later. "I don't know how he did it, but he gave me the slip."

Alex showed him the rifle, then said, "At least he's not armed."

Armstrong said, "Assuming things like that can get you killed. He could have a dozen other weapons in that trunk of his." Armstrong studied the barrel of the rifle, then said, "This could be the same rifle that was shot at you. Irene can take a look at it before we send it off to the state crime lab. What I don't get is why he did all this." Armstrong bit his lower lip, then asked, "Alex, do you think it's possible he's the one who took the emerald?"

Alex thought about it. "He had the same opportunity as my other guests. But it doesn't make sense for him to hang around after the murder. If he stole the emerald, why did he stay in Elkton Falls?"

"Maybe he thought it would be too suspicious if he took off too soon after the theft."

"That might be it, or it could be that he was after more than the Carolina Rhapsody," Alex said as he pointed to the marked map on top of the table near the bed. There was a small chunk of gold sitting on the map, and a circle marked around the orchard. "Patrick thought there was gold around here, but somebody was scamming him."

Alex explained Emma's belief that the analysis he'd found was falsified, though no doubt the gold was real enough. "My guess is that somebody sold him the location of a 'gold mine' for who knows how much money. He threw in some real gold to make it appear legitimate, and Thornton bit."

Elise said, "So he shot Vince to keep him away from the orchard, I can see that. But why did he shoot at us?"

"We were cleaning the lens a long time, so most likely he thought we were spying on him," Alex said. "You had my dad's binoculars, too, remember? If we'd spent as much time looking out as we did in, we might have spotted him digging on the property. It would be pretty hard to explain why a surveyor would be doing that."

"But if Thornton didn't know he was being cheated, why kill Cliff? And where's the emerald now? It doesn't make sense," Elise said.

Armstrong said, "She's got a point."

"I don't have it all figured out yet," Alex said. He thought a moment, then said, "You know, Cliff had a gold nugget in his pocket when he was murdered. I recently found out he was always looking for a way to get rich without earning it. What if he sold Thornton a fake claim to a vein of gold around here?"

The sheriff said, "It's possible, but I don't know how we'll prove any of it."

"When you find Thornton you can ask him. Is there any chance of tracking him down?"

"I've got my men on it, they're setting up roadblocks. Unless he knows the roads around here better than I think he does, we'll have him in an hour."

"Good, you can ask him then."

Long after Armstrong had cleared out and Alex went to bed, he found himself tossing and turning most of the night. Elise's doubts kept creeping into his thoughts, and the more he considered them, the more certain Alex became that he'd uncovered just a part of the story. There had to be more, but he couldn't put his finger on it until it was time to get up the next morning.

He awoke from his half-sleep with a start, suddenly realizing another way all the pieces actually fit together into a credible explanation. That's when Alex knew who was really behind the guard's murder and the theft of the Carolina Rhapsody emerald.

Now all he had to do was prove it.

20

Elise had already prepared everything for the breakfast but the muffins.

He asked, "Fiona hasn't come yet, has she?"

Elise said, "No, but she still has ten minutes. Do you think she's going to show up after what happened yesterday? I've got her check, but I don't know if she's going to come around to collect it."

Alex said, "I don't think she can afford not to. I need to make a call. If she comes, stall her until I get off the phone. It's important she doesn't leave."

"Alex, what's going on?"

"I think I figured something out, but I need Armstrong to check on something for me before I jump the gun."

Alex went into his office, keeping his door ajar so he could see the lobby while still having some privacy.

Armstrong was at his office, though it was not yet six-thirty.

From the sound of the man's voice, he'd most likely been up all night. "Alex, I'm glad you called. The state police just snagged Thornton on the Tennessee line. He should be back in Elkton Falls around lunchtime."

"That's good to hear, but I'm calling about something else. Did you ever track Cliff's ex-wife down?"

"No, I never could find her. Her name's Blanche Cliff, I don't have a maiden name for her. She seems to have dropped off the face of the earth."

"Do me a favor, go upstairs to the clerk's office and dig out a permit for me."

"Alex, Maggie will shoot me if I go digging through her files when she's not around."

"It's important," Alex said. "I'll hang on the line."

"I'm trusting you on this, Alex. What do you expect me to find?"

"If I'm right, you won't have to ask."

Alex waited nine minutes for the sheriff to get back on the line. Fiona still hadn't shown up, and Alex was wondering if she would. She had to, he kept telling himself. If she'd already bolted, they might never find her again.

The sheriff said, "Okay, I'm here. What's up?"

"Look at Fiona White's permit to peddle."

"Hang on a second." There was a break, then Armstrong said, "I've got it. Nothing odd about it that I can see."

Alex asked, "Is there a social security number on it? Run it through the system." Everything depended on his hunch, and the only way he'd be able to prove any of it was if she'd used her correct number. She had to have slipped up somewhere.

"I'll have to go back to my office to check this," the sheriff said.

Armstrong came on a minute later and said, "Nope, it's a fake. Looks like another dead end."

Alex felt his theory fall apart. Could he have been wrong? No, it was the only way everything made sense.

"Sheriff, do me one more favor. Pull up Cliff's ex-wife's social security number and compare the two."

"Alex, do you have any idea what you're doing?"

"I know I don't have any right to ask, but would you do it for me?"

The sheriff sighed, then said, "Hang on, I've got to go back downstairs."

The next time he came on the line, Armstrong said, "Son of a gun, how did you know?"

"Fiona said something about being at Denali, and one of Cliff's photographs showed a sign for Mount McKinley in the background with a woman cut from the picture. They're both the same place in Alaska, which is where the faked analysis came from."

"She faked the first five numbers, but she used the right last four. That can't be a coincidence. Now if we can just find her," the sheriff said.

Alex saw the front door open and Fiona White walked in. He said in a whisper, "She just walked into Hatteras West."

"Alex, if you're right, she's already killed one man. Don't do anything stupid. I'll get somebody out there fast."

Alex hung up the telephone and walked into the lobby to confront the murderer.

"Here are your muffins," Fiona said as she handed the last basket to Elise. The Muffin Lady turned to Alex and said, "Now I want my check."

Alex said, "I still have to cut it, we weren't sure you'd show up."

Elise looked surprised, but didn't say anything.

The Muffin Lady wasn't pleased with his answer. "The second I get my money, I'm gone forever, you can bank on that."

Alex glanced at the door, hoping to see one of Sheriff Armstrong's deputies, but there was no one there. He wanted to confront her, but Alex couldn't risk it. There were lives besides his own at stake. The most he could do was stall her long enough for them to capture her.

Blast it all, three guests were coming down the stairs for their breakfasts. Alex couldn't afford to put them in jeopardy too, but he still had to stall if he could.

"It'll just take a second," he said as he walked toward his office. Alex kept staring out the window, willing the sheriff's deputy to come speeding up Point Road.

There must have been something about his expression, because Fiona looked behind her, then said, "You know what? Forget it. You can mail it to me."

"I'll have it ready in a heartbeat," Alex said. He couldn't let her go. "Why don't you come back with me to the office?" That would get her away from his guests, and more importantly, take Elise out of immediate danger.

"I can't wait," Fiona said, then hurried for the door. "Mail it to me."

"Wait a second, Blanche." Alex regretted the ploy of using her real name the second it parted his lips.

She hesitated, then said, "You've lost your mind. I'm getting out of here." Then she ran out the front door.

"What was that all about?" Elise asked.

"Fiona White is Cliff's ex-wife. She killed him and then stole the Carolina Rhapsody. I just hope she doesn't get away." Alex said. "Elise, I can't let her escape. I'm going after her."

Alex found Fiona trying to start her car, frustrated by its failure to respond.

"Having some trouble?" he asked her.

Fiona replied by jutting a handgun out the window. "Give me the keys to your truck."

"You can't get away. The sheriff knows everything that happened. Give up."

"I don't think so," she said. "On second thought, I've got a better idea. You're going to drive me. There's nothing like a hostage to clear the way."

She shoved the gun in Alex's back after she got out of her car. "Don't do anything stupid and you won't get hurt."

Alex was heading toward his truck, cursing himself for letting her snare him so easily, when he heard a voice behind him. "I'm afraid I can't let you go."

Skip was standing there in the open, a gun trained on Fiona's back. As she whirled to face him, Alex dove behind his truck. He heard a pair of shots fired almost at the same time, and looked up quickly, not sure what he was going to find.

Fiona was on the ground clutching her leg, but she'd managed to hit Skip, as well. Though he stood his ground, there was blood seeping from his shoulder. Alex rushed to him, but he said, "Get her gun. I'm okay."

Alex retrieved the weapon. Fiona, or Blanche, as she was properly named, wasn't a threat to anyone, not with a bullet in her leg. Alex raced back to Skip. "I'm going to call an ambulance. I'm glad you were here."

"I had to make up for the night before, didn't I? When I heard Thornton got away, I had to believe there was more going on than we knew about."

Elise raced over to Alex, and after he assured her that he was unarmed, he asked her to call for an ambulance. Skip was starting to sag, so Alex took the gun from his hand and supported the man with his own weight. "It's a lucky thing her car wouldn't start," Alex said.

Skip managed a smile. "Luck had nothing to do with it. I pulled off all of her spark plug wires."

"How did you know she was dangerous?" Alex asked.

"Before she came into the inn, I saw her check the gun in her handbag. I would have rushed in if there'd been any trouble inside, but I thought the safest way to play it was to wait out here and see what happened."

"I'm glad you were around," Alex said.

They heard the ambulance right after hearing the police siren. "That's music to my ears," Skip said. "All those years on the force and I never even got shot at, then this happens. I think I'll let Armstrong handle Elkton Falls after all. I'm retiring for good this time."

The big man stayed on his feet until the EMS folks made him lie down on the gurney. A second ambulance was called for Blanche Cliff. There was no way they were going to make the ex-cop and the killer ride side by side.

Alex and Armstrong approached Blanche as she lay on the ground. Elise joined them a minute later. After the sheriff read Blanche her rights, he said, "You really hold a grudge, don't you? I can't believe you waited all that time to kill your ex-husband."

"You idiot, you have no idea what happened."

"So why don't you tell me."

Blanche said, "It was Cliff's idea from the start. He was looking for one big score so he could retire in style. I told him he was an idiot for selling that gold mine idea, but he wouldn't listen to me. That wasn't going to be enough for him, so he cooked up the robbery, too. I had the fake emerald made, and we were going to swap it out just before Reston Shay came to get it. I was supposed to tap Cliff hard enough to raise a welt, so it would look like he got taken by surprise."

"But you decided not to share, so you used the letter opener instead."

"He got exactly what he deserved," Blanche said.

"So where's the emerald?" Armstrong asked. "You know we're going to find it sooner or later."

"Good luck. It's hidden pretty well."

Armstrong laughed. "Don't worry, we're good at finding things. And if we don't, I've got a feeling there's an insurance man with a three-million-dollar reason to figure out what you did with it."

The second ambulance came and treated the woman's leg before loading her in the back bay. Armstrong said, "If you don't mind, I'll ride along with you'all."

After they were gone, Alex said, "It's hard to believe all this heartache stemmed from one man's greed."

Elise said, "I don't want to speak ill of the dead, but he harvested what he sowed, didn't he?"

"Let's go inside. We've got guests expecting us."

Elise said, "Before we go in, there's something we need to talk about."

Alex asked, "Is it about us?"

"It is," Elise said solemnly. "I'm ready to answer your question."

Alex found himself holding his breath in anticipation as he waited for his fate to be decided.

"Go ahead, I'm ready."

Elise said, "Alex, you've been the best friend I've ever had, and the thought of losing what we have right now is more than I can take."

He started to say something, but she held up one hand. "Please, just hear me out."

He nodded, not trusting himself to speak.

"I love Hatteras West almost as much as you do, and the thought of being forced to leave because something has broken between us is unbearable. And let's face it, my track record with relationships isn't all that sterling. I'm sorry, but I know this is true about myself. All the signs point to us staying friends. There's just too much to risk losing."

Alex felt his heart explode in his chest, but he fought to keep from showing his devastation. He knew on one level that what she said was true, all of it; it still didn't make it any easier to accept.

Elise took a deep breath, then added, "That said, if you're willing to risk everything, then so am I."

It took him a second to realize that he'd just heard what she said. "Excuse me?"

She laughed slightly. "I said I'd love to pursue a relationship with you, starting right now."

Alex said, "Are you sure?"

"Oh, Alex, I think we've talked this to death. Let's just take a chance."

And then she kissed him.